MURDERS

Killing Time

Anne Cassidy

■SCHOLASTIC

Scholastic Children's Books,
Commonwealth House, 1-19 New Oxford Street,
London WC1A 1NU, UK
a division of Scholastic Ltd
London ~ New York ~ Toronto ~ Sydney ~ Auckland
Mexico City ~ New Delhi ~ Hong Kong

First published in the UK by Scholastic Ltd., 1999

ISBN 0 439 01209 0

Typeset by TW Typesetting, Midsomer Norton, Somerset
Printed by Cox and Wyman Ltd, Reading, Berks.

10 9 8 7 6 5 4 3 2 1

Contents

1

The Long Drop

There were a lot of witnesses when Kelly Ford fell from the top of Huxley Point at 2.14 on the first of May. The good weather had brought people out of the dilapidated tower block and into the sunshine. People were letting their dogs run wildly in the surrounding waste ground; mums were watching toddlers on their tricycles; groups of teenage boys were kicking an old football about. There was even an ice cream van parked, taking advantage of the unseasonal warmth to sell a few lollies.

The tower block was sixteen storeys high and Kelly came from the top like a bird. That's what some of the witnesses said. One minute they were walking, chatting, eating, and the next they found themselves with their heads bent back looking up at the sky, at the girl plummeting down towards them.

It was quick, apparently. Just seconds from the moment she left the concrete edge to the point where she hit the ground. I imagined a collective gasp from the people, eyes closing, hands shielding the children, a lot of people turning away. There was a burst of silence. A single moment's quiet and a couple of dozen people frozen on the landscape as a sixteen-year-old girl flew through the sky.

After the deadening thump no one moved.

A slightly built girl in black leggings lay on the concrete slabs. Her hands and arms seemed to move for a couple of seconds, the police reports said, but it wasn't a sign of life. People everywhere looked away. A pretty blonde girl falling sixteen storeys on to the cold, hard, ungiving ground is not a nice thing to see.

I would probably have turned away if I had been there. I would have flinched, gasped, choked back an exclamation, looked back at the sky from where she came. But I wasn't there to see the girl or hear the thin wail of someone crying as pandemonium broke loose and children ran screaming for help. I heard that the ice cream man, in his panic to radio for help, inadvertently pressed the PLAY button and the music from Popeye the Sailor Man sounded across the estate.

I wasn't a witness, but I should have been. Kelly

Ford had been in touch with me a few days before she died. She'd asked for my help and I'd put her off. I'd been busy and hadn't taken it seriously enough.

By the time I heard about her death it was too late.

I should start at the beginning. A letter came for me on the Friday before Kelly Ford died. It was the day that I was supposed to be taking my boyfriend, Billy, to the airport. He was going to work abroad for a year and I was feeling apprehensive and disgruntled. To be honest my emotions were like jelly. A year seemed a whole lifetime; a summer holiday, a birthday, a Christmas, a Valentine's day away. A year when I'd be trudging round the grey streets of East London while he was working a hair's breadth away from tropical rain forests. I was upset.

I'd only gone into work to tidy up and make a few phone calls. The letter was in the middle of the pile that the postman cheerfully dropped into the office. On the front were the words, *Anthony Hamer Investigations Inc, Attention Ms Patsy Kelly*. I picked it out and looked at it for a minute.

It was unusual to receive a letter that was addressed to me personally. I'd worked in my uncle's detective agency for almost two years. I'd done just about every job there was to do; typist, filing clerk, receptionist, tea maker, shopper and phone-answerer. More recently I'd been helping my uncle with cases, following up insurance claims or missing persons and even some marital disputes. I'd got involved in some unpleasant murder cases and been in personal danger once or twice. Embarrassing though it was, I'd had my name in the newspaper as a kid detective who had got lucky and solved a crime. Even so, I rarely got post that was specifically addressed to me.

It was a white envelope with neat handwriting on the front. I pushed my thumb in the corner and tore it open. Inside was a short note. *Dear Miss Kelly*, it said, *You don't know me but I read about you in the local paper. I am in real trouble and I don't know who to turn to. Someone is stalking me and I'm afraid for my own safety. I need some help but I can't go to the police. Please contact me at the phone number below and I'll tell you about it. I've got money so I can pay you, Kelly Ford*.

I dialled the number and there was no answer. I rang it again thirty minutes later, just as I was preparing to leave the office. I stood and let it ring twenty times before giving up. I put the phone down and picked up the letter. Perplexed, I looked at my watch. It was nearly eleven o'clock and I was collecting Billy at eleven thirty. I grabbed a pad of Post-Its and left a message for Tony.

URGENT. Can you follow this up? I have to get Billy to his flight on time.

I underlined the URGENT three times, stuck it

on the letter and put it on Tony's desk. He was due in after lunch and could look into it then.

Whatever. I was in a hurry. I closed the office up and Kelly Ford went completely out of my mind. Instead I was thinking of Billy, in Africa for a year. I thought of his shirts and shorts folded up inside a case that had an Angola sticker on it and something deflated slowly inside my ribcage.

I drove up in a small black VW Golf. Billy struggled out to the car with a couple of giant zip-up bags, and a rucksack over his shoulder.

"Where are your suitcases?" I said.

"This is it. I won't need much," he said, putting them into the back of the car.

He was wearing jeans and a long-sleeved T-shirt. Around his waist he had an organizer belt that we'd found in a department store a few days earlier. It was like a big money belt, only it had compartments for passport, airline tickets, money, keys and important papers. It was black and each little pouch had Velcro fastenings. Billy loved it and had spent hours deciding what to put in each bit.

"It's so well designed," he kept saying.

While in the shop I'd bought him a small inflatable pillow for his long plane journey. When I gave it to him he'd looked at it in a puzzled sort of way. I'd felt embarrassed as if I'd bought something silly but when we got back to his house he'd blown it up and we'd played around with it. After a while though, he put it down and picked up the organizer belt again, marvelling at the little secret pockets that would hold so many things.

"It's just so well designed," he said again, shaking his head with wonder.

That was typical of Billy. Something solid and practical interested him much more than something frivolous. But then he always had been much older than his years. After his mum and dad had been killed in a car accident he'd had to do a lot of growing up, and some of his friends said that he was old before his time.

I cared for him a lot. An awful lot. We'd been friends for years before we got together.

"Are you going to drive at this speed the whole way to the airport?" Billy said, half jokingly.

"I thought we agreed that you weren't going to pass any more comments on my driving?"

"It's the car I feel sorry for," he said, a broad smile on his face.

"Enough," I said sharply, giving him a half-smile back.

But he had stopped paying attention and was running his fingers over the dashboard with pride.

A couple of weeks earlier I had finally passed my driving test. Billy had been with me and we'd been driving this black Golf that he had bought as a wreck and spent weeks doing up.

When I waved my pass certificate delightedly at him he grinned and took a wallet of papers out of the glove compartment. There was a registration document with the name Patricia Kelly written on it. I almost cried with pleasure. He pointed out the car's features to me as though he was a showroom salesman; all the time I was saying *ooh* and *ah!* There were extras as well; a small fire extinguisher, a set of spanners, a monkey wrench and a pair of fluffy dice to hang over the rear view mirror. I told him it was the best thing anyone had ever given me.

We arrived at the airport in good time. We both busied ourselves with practical things, buying sweets and magazines for the journey, looking up the flight information. He told me again how worthwhile the year would be, even though I'd heard it before.

"I'll be stationed in this new community centre that's been built, working with people who want to work on cars or engines of any sort. It won't just be young kids but older people too. I'll be living in the compound attached to it."

I nodded positively with half an eye on the TV monitors that gave the flight information. Eventually, when we'd talked ourselves dry, a notice came up saying his flight was boarding.

We stood looking at each other, and I didn't know what to say.

"It's not such a long time," he said, looking hard at me.

"No, course it's not," I said, nodding.

Then he kissed me on the forehead and hugged me into his chest.

I didn't wait to watch the plane take off. I just wanted to get out of the airport and on the road. It seemed to me that the year long clock would only start ticking as soon as I'd actually stopped seeing him.

I went back to his house after the airport. He'd asked me to think about living there when he was away, but I wasn't sure. When I walked into the kitchen the first thing I noticed was the inflatable pillow which he'd left on the side. He'd forgotten it and now he would have to sit through the eleven hour plane journey without any way to rest his head.

I sat down at the kitchen table and cried silently.

On Monday morning I went straight to this insurance firm that my uncle Tony did business with and picked up a couple of claims to assess. I took my time going back to the office and walked through the Exchange shopping centre, stopping to look at summer clothes. I got back to work after lunch and found my uncle working busily on his computer. By his side was a doorstep sandwich and a doughnut. He'd recently lost a lot of weight and had stopped dieting.

"I'm developing a webpage for the agency," he said, without looking at me.

"Did you get that message I left you on Friday?" I said, remembering the letter.

"I got held up on Friday, so I didn't get back."

"Oh."

I shuffled through my uncle's papers and saw the letter with the Post-It still attached. I went back into my own office and rang the telephone number again and stood listening while it rang endlessly. I found myself getting irritated so I replaced the receiver and sat down. All I had was a name and a phone number that did not answer. How on earth did Kelly Ford expect me to get in touch with her? I had no idea what to do about it. I left it in my pending tray intending to speak to Tony about it later.

The phone call came at about four o'clock in the afternoon.

"Good afternoon. Anthony Hamer's Detective Agency. How may I help?"

I said it in my nicest voice and was ready to take notes in case it was a new client.

"Patsy, it's Heather Warren here."

"Oh, hi. How are you?" I said, pleased. Heather was a CID Inspector that I knew.

"Not so wonderful. I've just been down to Huxley Point. A sixteen-year-old girl has just fallen off the top. Jumped or pushed, we don't know."

"Oh."

"Thing is, she had a piece of paper in her pocket with your name on it. I should say your name and the address of your uncle's agency."

My eye strayed across my desk and rested on the

letter with the Post-It stuck to it. The letter that I had had for three days and hadn't done anything about.

"The kid's name is Kelly Ford. Sound familiar?"

Kelly Ford. I put the palm of my hand over my mouth and closed my eyes.

Someone is stalking me and I'm afraid for my own safety.

"Yes, it does." I said, glumly.

She'd asked me for help and I'd been too busy with my own problems.

2

Kelly Ford

My uncle Tony was furious with me. He banged a packet of Hobnob biscuits down on to my desk.

"Someone asked for help and protection and you left it over the weekend!"

"I left it for you to look into. You said you were coming back on Friday afternoon and I put it on your desk."

My temper was rising. I had done all I could. How could it be my fault? My uncle took a great breath and started to speak.

"Rule number one. If someone contacts the agency and tells us that they might be in actual danger we do something about it immediately."

"I did!"

"No, you made a phone call, then dropped it."

"You weren't here!" I raised my voice and stood with my jaw clenched, looking my uncle straight in the face.

"Rule number two," he said after a few seconds' silence, "If you can't deal with it, pass it on to one of our freelances. Or to another agency. You don't leave someone in trouble to look out for themselves. This girl called for help and you didn't answer her. You could have made a difference to her, Patricia. All the difference in the world."

I watched his office door shut lightly behind him and sat for what seemed like a long time. Then I reached across and took a Hobnob biscuit from the packet and nibbled at it miserably.

A couple of hours later I was in the local police station sitting across the desk from my friend, Detective Inspector Heather Warren. She was sympathetic.

"These things happen, Patsy. It's an error of judgement. It happens to all of us at some time or another."

I'd known Heather since I started working at my uncle's agency. I'd become involved in some of her cases and I knew that she liked me. I should have felt a bit better but instead there was this growing sicky feeling near my ribs. I looked at her while she scanned the letter that I'd brought. She read it from top to bottom then read it again.

"My uncle is furious," I said, thinking of Tony's wretched expression.

She tutted loudly. Heather and my uncle didn't like each other.

"Like he's never made any mistakes. Like he's perfect," she said.

I managed a half-smile and looked out through the glass partition to the rest of the CID office. There were some familiar faces there, and a few I'd never seen before. On the far wall I noticed that the white display board had been cleared of pictures and notices. A woman was spraying liquid on to it and rubbing small circles with a cloth.

It would be the central information board for the investigation, I knew. Within the next few hours it would be covered with relevant documents. There would be pictures of the dead girl as she lay on the concrete at the foot of the tower block. Within a short while they would have pictures of Kelly Ford when she had been alive. Side by side they would be like a gruesome make-over. The photographs would eventually be surrounded by felt-tip handwriting; details of the scene of crime, maps, diagrams, suspects, last known movements.

I turned back to see Heather tapping on her computer keyboard.

"Do you know what happened to Kelly Ford?" I said.

Heather turned to face me and for the first time I

noticed how tired she looked. Her hair was tousled as though she'd not combed it that day, and the roots were darker than the rest. More than that, I noticed something that almost made me smile. She was wearing odd earrings. Oh, they were similar, each with three small balls hanging from the lobe, but they were different earrings, one metallic and one wooden.

Heather was usually so well presented, so perfectly dressed and made-up. I knew how much it galled some of the other officers, especially the male ones, that a competent and attractive woman in her early thirties had been promoted above them. There wasn't usually a hair out of place. I wondered what was wrong.

"I'll tell you what I know, Patsy, but before I do, we must get some ground-rules here. On no account are you to take part in this investigation. This is a full scale murder inquiry and if I hear that you've been doing any sniffing around on your own then you and I will fall out."

I nodded rapidly.

Heather's voice became business-like and brisk.

"Kelly Ford was sixteen, in her last year of school. She lived in Stratford, a bus ride or so away from Huxley Point. The only family member we've spoken to so far is her brother, Raymond. Her mother is too upset, you can imagine."

I nodded.

"Her brother said that she'd been depressed for a while. Apparently she'd got involved with her best friend's cousin, Vincent Black. He's a nasty piece of work. We've got some paperwork on him. He's in prison for GBH at this very moment."

"So, he's not a suspect ?"

"Not exactly, no. Let me explain. Six months ago this Vincent Black, his cousin and Kelly Ford went into a jeweller's. There was a customer in there, a man called Dan Mackenzie. He was picking up his girlfriend's watch or bracelet or something. An argument broke out and then punches were thrown. It's all on the shop's videotape. This Dan Mackenzie fell to the ground and the threesome left. Mackenzie got up, left the shop and a couple of hours later he collapsed and had to be taken to hospital. Three weeks later he died. He was only twenty-three."

"Oh," I said.

"Vincent Black can't be charged with murder, so he got twelve months for Assault and Grievous Bodily Harm. That was just after Christmas. Kelly Ford cried at the trial, but as soon as Vince started his prison sentence she cooled off."

"Had she met someone else?"

"Raymond's not sure. He says she spent an awful lot of time alone. The boyfriend, Vince, begged her to go and see him again, and she did. There was a row. He exploded and made a grab for her across the table. As he was dragged away he made threats to

15

her. It was all caught on videotape. Poor Vincent Black. Every time he puts a foot wrong there's a video camera pointed at him."

"So Kelly didn't go again?"

"No, that was it. A week or so ago she left her mum's place. She said she felt unsafe and was going to stay with a friend. We've still got to check into all that."

"What about the phone number? The one in the letter?"

"Raymond said that Kelly's mum gave her a mobile when she left home so that she could keep in touch. Apparently she did ring her a couple of times. Like I said, I haven't spoken to Mrs Ford yet."

"Could it have been suicide?" I said.

"We don't know for sure. At the moment we're looking at murder. Threats had been made to her and she was scared. She even wrote to you saying that she was being stalked. Then she falls off a building. I think it's too much of a coincidence to say that she committed suicide.

The telephone rang and Heather picked it up. She looked away from me and I could hear her saying *Mm? Mm?*

I found myself sitting back in the chair and wondering about Huxley Point. Why there? Did Kelly have friends in that area? Why that particular building?

Heather was nodding as well as murmuring into

16

the phone. Her expression was strained and I noticed her long fingernails digging into the edge of the table.

"Right … right, get back to me," she said, replacing the receiver.

"Well?" I said.

"That was the path lab. They're still doing tests. There are the obvious injuries that she sustained from the fall and there's some bruising on the upper arm which could suggest that she had been grabbed or pulled along."

"There was no sighting of any other person?"

"None reported. My officers have started a thorough search of the building as well as door-to-door inquiries. We should know more after that."

Heather was running her hands through her already messy hair and drawing in air through her nostrils as though she'd just surfaced from underwater.

"Are you all right?" I said. "You don't look well."

"Yes," she said, waving her hand dismissively. "It's just that sometimes this job gets me down. This is one of those times."

She looked fuller as well, as though she'd put weight on. Her eyes were puffy and the buttons of her blouse pulled tightly across her chest.

"You look tired."

"I'm not sleeping very well at the moment. Anyway, enough of this. I've got a case to follow."

She leaned over and fiddled with the mouse on her computer. I stood up to go.

"I know this isn't my business, and I've got no intention of getting involved, but could you let me know if there are any developments? Only I feel bad about the girl."

"If anything substantial comes in I'll let you know. Unofficially, I mean."

"Thanks Heather."

I left her office and walked through the CID office, busier now. I glanced over at the whiteboard. Someone had written the words KELLY FORD MURDER across the top. I nodded to a couple of people that I knew and left.

MURDER. It was still a word that made my neck tingle with anxiety.

3

Rest In Peace

Kelly Ford's funeral was ten days later. I'd watched the time in between creep by, each day seeming slower than the one before. My uncle Tony had been tied up in some insurance work and I spent most of my time in the office. The atmosphere had been icy, with him dropping several comments on the subject of *people needing to take their work seriously*.

Things weren't much better at home. My mum and her live-in boyfriend were getting ready for their wedding at the beginning of June. Every time I walked through the front door she seemed to be on the phone to the florists or the caterers or the dressmakers. Her boyfriend, a mature student called Gerry, spent most of his time sitting on the settee blinking happily through his round glasses, his hands clasped in satisfaction across his bulging belly.

So I sat at my desk and did as much paperwork as I could. When I'd finished I tidied the filing cabinet and added some new clients to the database. I cleaned up, descaled the office kettle and shopped for tea bags, coffee and pink wafer biscuits. When it was all done I sat and thought about Kelly Ford and wondered whether the police had any suspects. I kept taking my mobile phone out of my bag and looking hard at it, willing it to ring, hoping that Heather would be able to tell me that they'd arrested somebody, and that the case was wrapped up.

It stared silently at me though, day after day, with not a single call. I found myself checking the batteries, ringing up the speaking clock just to make sure that it was still working.

When I wasn't wishing for Heather to ring I was waiting for a letter from Billy. After he'd been gone about a week I found myself watching down the street for the postman and feeling disappointed when no airmail envelope dropped on to the hall mat.

Billy had told me that he would write when he could.

"As soon as I'm set up in my placement I'll write and give you my address. If it's an emergency you should ring the London office and they'll get a direct line through to someone who can contact me."

The day before he left he'd bought me an airmail pad and a packet of envelopes. They were light blue with dark blue and red piping round the edge. We were sitting side by side on the settee in his living room.

"I could have bought these!" I'd said.

"I know. But this way there'll be no excuse for you not writing."

"Of course I'll write," I said, feeling the lightness of the envelopes and the tissue feel of the writing paper.

"Make sure you don't get too involved in some exciting case and forget about me."

He put his fingers on my shoulder and started to trace small circles. I sat very still for a moment and felt a tingle shoot across my chest.

"As if I could," I whispered, and felt his mouth on my neck as the pad and envelopes slipped off the settee and on to the floor.

After a while he leaned down and picked them up.

"I know you," he said, "you'll get involved in some murder case and I'll be the last thing on your mind."

"I won't," I said, a feeling of foreboding starting to settle.

I could have gone to Africa with him. He'd asked me, even begged me to. A year's voluntary service abroad. The two of us working on some project, helping other people instead of sitting in our comfortable homes just thinking of ourselves.

I'd said no. I'd hadn't wanted to take a year away from my job.

Sitting in the office, tidying away the cups and saucers and putting the biscuits into the tin I wondered why on earth I hadn't gone. The one case that might have been worth staying behind for had come too early, had slipped through my fingers, had shown me to be half-hearted and not very good at my job.

Africa. Now, when it was too late, it sounded like a good place to go.

I got to the church early and sat at the back. I had no actual right to be at Kelly Ford's funeral. I hadn't known the girl, but still I felt moved by her death. I wasn't religious and didn't have any prayers to say, but I felt it was right that I should be there. I had bought some white lilies and laid them in the foyer of the church with the other flowers.

I watched as the mourners arrived. They came in small groups, walking hesitantly up the aisle, their heels tapping on the floor, waving at others who they recognized. Up in front, on high legs, sat the coffin. On top of it was a single wreath of multicoloured blooms.

Moments later there was a burst from the organ and after a couple of uncertain notes a tune sounded.

That's when I saw a woman of about forty walking slowly but stoutly up the aisle linking arms with a young man of about twenty. The woman's face was drawn, her mouth held rigidly in a half-moon shape. The young man's face was red as though he'd been crying and his lips were crumpled up.

Kelly Ford's mother and her brother, I thought. I caught the woman's eye for a split second before she passed me. It was hard look. An *angry* look.

After the service had been going on for a few minutes I noticed Heather Warren and another officer entering. I recognized the man. It was Des Murray, a CID officer who worked in Heather's team. He was not my favourite person and he gave a scowl and whispered something to Heather when he saw me. She came straight over to where I was sitting.

"What are you doing here?" she hissed. "I thought we agreed that you were not going to be involved?"

"I'm not," I said, louder than I intended. "I'm just here for the funeral."

A couple of people looked round at us disapprovingly. Heather sat back on the seat, emitting a long sigh. After a few seconds she moved quietly along the pew and walked over to the other side of the church.

I watched her go. She had a long cream mac on, which looked wrinkled and grubby. Her hair was hooked behind her ears, flicking up behind where it had outgrown the style which she usually wore. She didn't look anything like the smart, dynamic woman that I had worked with in the past.

The sermon was dull. The mourners seemed to be getting restless and a few of them were yawning and looking at their watches.

Then I heard the sound of high heels tapping on the floor behind me. I looked round, with most of the back row of the congregation. A tall, red-haired girl in a very short black dress was standing in the middle of the aisle. She had a shoulder bag which hung from her left shoulder down to her right hip. After a second's hesitation she walked up the aisle, her heels dragging and scraping along. She went in a row or two in front of me, and I could see other mourners eyeing her and nudging each other.

I looked across to Heather and saw her talking quietly with Des Murray, her hand cupping her mouth, her eyes on the new arrival.

The service was over a short while later. I waited for the coffin to be carried down the aisle. Directly behind it was Mrs Ford, who was walking beside a thin young woman with closely cropped hair. She seemed unsteady on her feet and put her hand out for the young woman's arm. Her son, Raymond, was further back, walking by himself amid the rest of the mourners.

Once outside the bright daylight made me blink a couple of times, and I found myself on a narrow pavement being hustled by the crowd. Some of the mourners were trying to get to the black cars and others were chatting with people they hadn't seen for a while.

I edged through the crowd and found myself about a metre away from the redhead who was talking animatedly to a couple of people. Even though she was wearing a black dress, she seemed out of place. Her hair was a little too bouncy, her body language a little too loose. In her fingers she was holding an unlit cigarette, and I noticed that her nails were long and shaped, and painted a fluorescent pink colour.

Mrs Ford seemed to notice it as well. She was just about to get into a black limousine when she caught sight of the redhead. The girl turned round to look at her.

"I don't know what you're doing here, young lady!" Mrs Ford said loudly, like a teacher annoyed with a difficult pupil.

A hush fell on the crowd and everyone turned to look.

The redhead's forehead creased and her mouth dipped. She walked dramatically across to Mrs Ford and buried her head in the woman's shoulder. Mrs Ford seemed to take a deep breath and her mouth puckered with uncertainty. After a couple of seconds she lifted one of her arms and gently moved the girl away from her.

"Not now, Carly," I heard her say.

The redhead gave a couple of sobs and walked off

back to the crowd that she'd been standing with. Mrs Ford and her son got into the car. The door of the car slammed shut and the mourners turned back into their own groups, and immediately began to talk again.

I was feeling awkward, on my own, wondering what to do, when I noticed the woman who had helped Mrs Ford in the church standing by herself a couple of metres away. She was about my age, I thought. I was about to go and talk to her when Heather Warren walked over and stood beside me. Des Murray, thankfully, was nowhere to be seen.

"I take it the redhead with the long legs was Kelly's best friend?" I said, nodding over at the girl who had just been rebuffed by Mrs Ford.

"Yes. Carly Dickens. I don't think Mrs Ford or Raymond ever liked Carly. They thought she was a bad influence on Kelly. I don't think she's that fond of them either."

"Have you got anywhere yet?" I said quietly, not wanting to seem too pushy.

"Nope. But don't quote me on that. We've done the legwork. We've knocked on doors. We've talked to family and friends. We're currently following several lines of inquiry. That's what you'll see in the press releases. Truthfully though, we're no closer than we were on the day she died."

"Somebody must have seen her though. It was broad daylight!" I said.

Most of the mourners were leaving and a couple of men were loading the wreaths into the back of the last black car. Des Murray had appeared from nowhere and was chatting to the driver. He threw a look of annoyance in my direction.

Heather's voice lowered and she spoke in a sing-song tone.

"No member of the public saw her arrive at Huxley Point. Nobody in the flats saw her waiting for the lifts or walking up the stairs. Nobody saw her go on to the roof."

"I find that really odd," I said, truthfully.

"It's one of those tower blocks that they're going to demolish, so it's only half full. Most of the residents are in the lower floors. The roof door was hanging open, probably had been for months. It's a really run down place."

"What about her mum and her brother? Did you speak to them?" I said, as the back door slammed on the last car. All the mourners had gone and Des Murray was leaning against a parked car tapping his foot idly on the pavement. Heather gave a great sigh and ran her fingers through her hair.

"They're an odd couple. Mrs Ford doesn't seem very stable and Raymond isn't very communicative. He was a loner, spent a lot of time hanging around with his sister. They don't say a lot and I've got a feeling that they're holding stuff back. I don't want to push them too hard though. They're grieving. I'll just bide my time. Keep talking to them. Family secrets usually have a way of coming out."

I was about to say something when Heather put her hand over her mouth.

"Excuse me, Patsy, I'm not feeling very well…"

She walked abruptly away with her head bowed and disappeared into the church. When I looked round Des Murray was beside me, his hands in his pockets.

"Miss Kelly, have you been upsetting Inspector Warren?"

I ignored him and looked agitatedly around. I wondered if I should go after her. I was about to do it when she reappeared with a large wad of tissues in her hand. She didn't look any better.

"Are you all right?" I said when she got closer.

"I'm fine. Just a bit under the weather."

Des Murray was looking at his watch.

"We should go," Heather said, "They'll be at the cemetery now. Can we give you a lift?"

"No, I've got to get back to work," I said.

It wasn't true but I wouldn't have felt right going to the cemetery. I watched as they walked off towards their car then I got my car keys out and headed off in the direction of mine.

All the time I was thinking about Huxley Point. On a bright spring day someone took a sixteen-year-old girl to the top of a tower block and threw her off. And nobody saw a thing.

It didn't make any sense.

4

Relationships

The next morning when I went down to breakfast, there was an icy atmosphere. Both my
mum and her boyfriend, Gerry, were in the kitchen.

"Morning!" I said, my voice light.

"Morning," Gerry said, his voice flat.

"Good morning," my mum said, her words crisp.

I busied myself getting some slices of bread out of
the freezer and hummed along to some music on the
radio. It was obviously a lovers' tiff. I wondered what
had happened. Just lately my mum and Gerry had
been inseparable. I'd entered the living room on
several occasions and found them draped across each
other or stuck together in some ravenous kiss. Not
that they were shamefaced about it. Instead of sitting
up, pink with embarrassment, as I would have been,
they both usually collapsed in a heap of laughter.

Since the wedding had been arranged the house was in constant flux. There was a never-ending stream of friends visiting to congratulate them or find out about the arrangements: the registry office, the hall, the food, the table settings, the music, the flowers. Once or twice I'd come in late in the evening and found Gerry with his friends in the living room and my mum with a couple of her friends in the kitchen, leaving me feeling like an intruder in my own home.

Not that I was all that keen on spending time submerged in the wedding arrangements. Since they'd announced their plans I had deliberately kept out of the way as much as possible, spending a lot of time out with Billy or in my own room. I'd even considered going to stay with my dad in Birmingham for a couple of weeks, but had decided against it in the end.

Since Billy had departed for Africa the forthcoming wedding seemed to take possession of every room of the house: the reply cards, the early gifts, the table decorations, the boxes of wine, the lists of things to do. In my own room hung my mum's outfit which wasn't to be seen by Gerry. I was greatly relieved to see that it wasn't a long white dress with a veil and tiara. Even the talk about the wedding seemed louder, more frantic, as though someone had turned the volume up.

It seemed as though I couldn't walk into a single room without the wedding forcing itself at me. It was like a giant inflatable that had had its string pulled and was slowly unfolding and filling up all the space in the house.

"Could you pass me the jam, Pats?" I heard Gerry's voice.

Without a word I reached into the cupboard and got out the jam. I resolved to tell him, seriously, to stop calling me Pats once and for all. He was the only person in the world who did so and it was most annoying.

"Hand me the skimmed milk, Patsy love." My mum's voice came from the end of the table that was furthest away from Gerry.

I opened the fridge and got it out. As I passed it to her I noticed her stony expression.

"What's the matter?" I said quietly, looking from my mum to Gerry and back again.

"Your mum's upset because I've decided to give up college and get a job."

I raised my eyebrows in surprise. For as long as I'd known him Gerry had been a mature student, his head buried in books and his arm permanently resting on the college bar. It was where they'd met: my mum in her smart suits, carrying her shiny lecturer's briefcase; Gerry, his jeans and shirts never quite meeting at his waist.

"Tell her which job," my mum demanded, shaking the newspaper rigorously and then pretending to read it.

"It's in *The Bull's Head*. It's only bar work but it'll bring in some money. I've told your mother I'm fed up with sponging off her."

"I'm supporting you! There's a world of difference. You're two years into your degree. Another year and you'll have letters after your name! Then you'll be able to get a proper job, with a salary, pension, paid holidays, all the perks. Isn't that right, Patsy?"

My mum looked at me expectantly. She wanted me to agree with her.

"Meanwhile you pay all the bills and I have to ask you for pocket money! It's not right. A man needs to be independent. What do you think, Patsy?"

Gerry gave me a sly look. He knew that I didn't approve of his living rent-free at our house. I'd made enough comments about it.

"But it's wasting what you've already done. Patsy, tell him. Another year and he could be set up for life!"

I looked from one to the other not knowing what to say. In all honesty I should have agreed with Gerry. On the other hand my mum had a point.

The sound of the phone warbling from the hall-way interrupted things.

"I'll get it," I said hastily, and took giant steps out of the room, shutting the door firmly behind me. The hallway was cool and hushed. I was grateful. I picked up the phone and heard a familiar voice.

"Patsy, is that you? It's Heather."

"Oh hi, how are you feeling?" I said, relieved that it was for me.

"A lot better."

"Shouldn't you go to a doctor?"

I heard Heather laugh and then there was a short silence. I thought for a minute that I'd been cut off.

"I know what's wrong. I'm pregnant. That's what's wrong."

"Oh," I said, and went silent.

"Are you there?"

"Yes, I didn't know … I didn't realize. Well, congratulations," I said.

"I don't think so, Patsy. It's not something I'm particularly pleased about."

"That's a shame," I said.

"I can't see a baby fitting into my lifestyle, can you? I mean, they don't have crèches in police stations."

"What about the father?"

"Long gone. Just one of those things. It didn't work out."

"But won't he want to know?"

"Nope. Believe me, he won't."

The kitchen door opened then and my mum came out into the hallway. She was talking rapidly. "You've spent all this time studying and you're going to throw it away to work in some dead end job. It makes me sick. It's a total waste of talent."

Gerry was following behind her, nodding his head wisely as if agreeing with a well made point.

"I suppose you're right. You've got a point, if you really don't mind me not working. It's not like I won't be able to pay you back, after all."

"What are you going to do?" I said to Heather, as they edged past me, my mum picking up her bag and car keys, Gerry grabbing a tatty cardboard folder.

"I don't know. I'm ten weeks gone, and I've been thinking and thinking."

My mum waved to me and Gerry gave me a kind of hopeless smile as if to say, *I tried Pats, honest, but she just won't let me work*.

"Are you thinking of an abortion?" I said, after the front door had shut.

"Yes. No. I don't know. Look, I have to go. I only really rang about all that Kelly Ford stuff we talked about. I don't need to tell you that it's confidential."

"No, course not," I said, mildly offended.

"See you soon," she said, and hung up.

Just then a series of letters came through the letterbox. I squatted down to sort through them. Several letters for my mum, a couple of bills and a letter for Gerry. No pale blue envelope with red and blue edging. No letter from Africa. No word from Billy. The disappointment was something I was getting used to.

I stood up. Heather Warren was pregnant. I tried to imagine her with a large oval stomach, or pushing a buggy down the street. Neither image came easily. I shoved the letters on the hall table and went upstairs.

5

Raymond Ford

I got to work early and had to open up the office and pick up the post. I switched on the kettle, the computer and the lights, in that order. I made myself a cup of tea and sat down to open the letters.

It was over two weeks since Billy had gone; just under that since Kelly Ford had been murdered. I gave a forced laugh. Billy had been worried about me being so involved in a case that I wouldn't remember to write to him. It seemed that the opposite had happened. I had nothing to investigate and was waiting for word from him. Billy was so busy he hadn't had a moment to sit down and write to me.

I took my glasses off and gave them a thorough clean. How long could it take for a letter to come from Africa?

A knock on the office door stopped me. It was only eight-forty-five and we weren't usually open that early. I put my glasses on and stood up, stretching my arms to the ceiling; then I smoothed my skirt down and went to the door.

A young man of about eighteen was standing there. He went to say something but then stopped, took out a piece of paper from his pocket and read my name off it.

"Patsy Kelly?"

"Yes," I said. He looked vaguely familiar.

"I'm Raymond Ford. My sister wrote to you before she…"

He left the sentence in mid-air and stood looking at me. His shoulders were rounded and he seemed to be leaning forward. Kelly Ford's brother. I remembered him from the funeral, walking up the aisle clinging on to his mother's arm.

"Come in," I said, holding the door open.

"I hope you don't mind me coming. Actually I wasn't sure what time you opened. I haven't got an appointment…"

His head was bent to one side and I had an urge to straighten him up, push his shoulders back.

"Have a seat. Let me get you a tea or coffee?"

"No, thanks. But don't let me stop you," he said, banging his knuckles together. "I don't want to be any trouble."

I poured some water on to a tea bag and got some

biscuits out of the tin. Part of me was puzzled by his presence; another part was intrigued.

"What can I do for you, Raymond?"

"It's about my sister."

Funny, I'd thought it might be.

"Only I saw you at the funeral, at least, I asked that lady Inspector about you, and I know that Kelly wrote to you before she…"

He stopped and I found myself speaking softly to him.

"Before she was killed. Raymond, I can't tell you how sorry I feel about it. I got her letter and tried to contact her. The next thing I knew she was dead."

There was a lot more I could have said, excuses I could have made, but I didn't.

"I know, the Inspector explained. Actually, it's been a long timc now and nobody's been caught. My mum's in a terrible state, she just doesn't sleep at night and I know she's drinking a lot."

"She's just lost her daughter. It's a difficult time."

"Yes."

He said it with a sigh and sat silently. I waited for his next words, wondering all the time what the point was.

"Raymond, why have you come to see me?"

"I thought about going to the police but they don't seem to be getting anywhere. So I thought, why not go to that woman? The detective?"

"What about?"

"I thought, Kelly would have wanted that. She picked you out of the newspapers after all. It was your name you see. *Kelly*. It's the same as hers."

Kelly shared the same name as me. It hadn't registered.

Raymond put his hand inside his jacket and pulled out a cassette tape. He held it in the air by a corner.

"It's Kelly," he whispered.

I looked at the cassette tape and then back at Raymond. Why had he brought this to me? What on earth was I supposed to do with it?

"It'll only take a minute to listen to it. It's not very long."

I frowned for a moment. Then I pulled open the bottom drawer of the filing cabinet and took out a cassette player. He handed me the tape and I put it in and pressed the play button. I picked up my tea and sipped it. As I looked over the top of my mug I could see him looking closely at the tape player. He had a smile on his face that made me feel uncomfortable.

"My name is Kelly Ford and er ... er ... I'm making this tape on the twenty-third of April. I'm leaving it in case ... well in case anything happens to me."

The voice was shaky and nervous. A sixteen-year-old girl who was scared.

"I got this problem. My ex-boyfriend Vince is inside and he's threatened me because I'm seeing someone else.

It's complicated, but some very odd things have been happening to me and I'm scared.

It wasn't my fault that Vince ended up in prison. Everything was fine until he smacked that kid in the jewellers. That's the thing about Vince, he always has to go too far. I know that he's got someone coming after me. I know that…"

There was a long pause, and I caught Raymond Ford's eye.

"There's more," he whispered, pointing to the player.

"There's this red car that keeps following me. On my way to school in the morning. I look round and I can see it. After school today I took a lot of care to make sure I wasn't being followed, and then I turned a corner and it was suddenly there. I think Vince has got someone keeping an eye on me. It's really spooking me.

And the phone calls, they're awful too. It's always when I'm on my own in the house. I pick up the receiver and there's just someone breathing. Then a voice starts saying two-timer, two-timer, over and over again.

I'd go to the police, but I'm scared. Look, it's like this. Maybe Vince is trying to scare me. Maybe that's enough revenge for him. Trouble is, if I go to the Law and he gets in more trouble, then he'll really have a reason to hurt me.

All I want to do is forget Vince and get on with my own life. Vince won't like it when he knows the truth. He won't like it at all."

"That's it," Raymond said.

"When did you find it?"

"A couple of days ago. I was clearing up some of Kelly's things. I was going to take it to the police, but then I changed my mind. I just don't think they're taking it seriously."

"I don't know what I can do about it," I said, puzzled.

"I've always been close to my sister. I've always felt responsible for her. Ever since she was young I've looked out for her. When Vince Black was sent to prison she confided in me."

I nodded.

"She told me that after Mackenzie died she never felt the same about Vince again. She felt scared of him. He'd actually *killed* someone. We never liked him, Mum and me. I think he was the one who killed her."

"But Vince was in prison when she died."

"I don't mean him personally. He has mates."

"Have you got someone in mind?"

"Liam Casey. He's Vincent's best mate. I saw him hanging round the house once or twice and he was around the school entrance a couple of times when I was picking Kelly up."

"Did you tell this to the police?"

"Not at the time. Kelly wouldn't let me. She said to ignore it."

"Do you know where this Liam Casey is?"

"Nope. I heard he moved out of the area when Vince got sent down."

Raymond folded his arms across his chest and sat back. I finished my tea and thought for a moment.

"Kelly was scared, but she wouldn't go to the police and she wouldn't let you go to the police. So she made this tape, then she left home and went into hiding."

"I got home one day and found her gone. She didn't even tell me where. It was as if she couldn't trust *anybody*."

Raymond screwed his lips up and looked closely at his fingernails.

"Did she tell you who her new boyfriend was?"

He shrugged moodily.

"I never bothered about her boyfriends. They came and went. I was always there for her. I was a friend to her as well as a brother."

He paused, and I remembered Kelly's other friend, the redhead with the long legs who'd been at the funeral.

"What about Carly Dickens? Do you think Kelly might have confided in her?"

He shook his head positively.

"She wouldn't have trusted Carly. Carly used to go out with Liam. She'd do anything for him. He dropped her a while back and she was always hanging round him, always talking about them getting back together. I'm sure that Kelly wouldn't have told Carly anything. I think I was the only person she could really trust. Once she moved out I never saw her again."

There was quiet as I let it all sink in.

"I can't do anything with this, Raymond. It's too big, and anyway it's being followed up by the police."

"They're dragging their feet. They're considering suicide, and that's not what happened."

He said it firmly, banging his knuckles together. His face had crumpled up again and he looked much younger than before. I agreed with him. I didn't think it was suicide either. For a moment I felt sorry for him.

"I'm on quite good terms with Detective Inspector Warren. Why don't you let me have this tape? I'll give it to her and tell her about your worries. I'm sure she'll treat it seriously. That's the sort of person she is."

Just then the office door opened and my uncle puffed in carrying a pile of files and books.

"I'm not as fit as I used to be, Patricia," he said and then noticed Raymond Ford.

"This is Kelly Ford's brother. You remember, the girl who wrote to me?"

"Of course," Tony said. "Terrible business. We were very sorry to hear about her sad death."

"I'll leave you my phone number," Raymond said, "in case you need to get in touch."

I passed him a piece of paper and he wrote slowly, forming each number carefully. I found myself twitching with impatience. My uncle gave a couple of coughs and disappeared into his office.

"You'll definitely speak to the Inspector?" he said, getting up and walking towards the door, his shoulders rounded.

"I'll do it, Raymond."

He pursed his lips and nodded his head. His eye caught mine for a minisecond and then he left. I sat at my desk holding the cassette tape, and tried to work out why I felt such relief that he'd gone. He was someone who cared about his dead sister and was trying to find out the truth. I ought to like him.

The problem was that I didn't.

6

Old Friends

I told Tony that I was going out for a while. Then I took the cassette, which I'd put into a padded envelope, and drove in the direction of the police station. I thought that it was important to go and see Heather as soon as possible. I had these peculiar feelings of guilt inside, as though I was responsible in some way for receiving the tape, and that I would be accused of poking my nose into the case. I wanted to pass it on without any delay.

A kilometre or so down the High Road I hit the tail end of a traffic jam. I found myself inching forward for a couple of hundred metres and then coming to a complete stop. I sat, like everyone else, for five or six minutes before I turned the engine off and opened my door to let the air in. There were buses, lorries and cars tightly packed for as far as the eye could see. Even the pedestrians were standing, looking in the direction of the jam. I considered turning round but when I looked there were a dozen or so vehicles behind me. There was nothing else for it but to wait.

That was when I saw Joey Hooper walking along the pavement in the opposite direction. He was on his own, talking into a mobile phone. He was wearing khaki trousers and a denim jacket and over his shoulder he had a rucksack.

"Joey!" I said, in a loudish voice. He walked on though, oblivious.

Joey Hooper was a black kid who I had met on a case the previous year. The last I'd heard of him was that he'd got six months in prison for Assault with a Deadly Weapon. People at the time said he'd been lucky to get such a short sentence. I hadn't agreed. He'd had a terrible time and lost his older brother who had died after a racist beating. I remembered liking him a lot.

"*JOEY!*" I shouted at the top of my voice.

He stopped and turned in my direction. He looked older than his eighteen years. For a few moments he searched quizzically up and down the stranded cars, then his eyes settled on me getting out of my car and his face broke into a smile. I gestured for him to come over. He said something into his mobile then put it into his rucksack.

"Patsy. You're looking all right."

"Joey! It's brilliant to see you. I didn't know you were … that you'd finished your … that they'd let you out of…"

"Prison. Say the word, Patsy. It won't bite you."

I shrugged in a silly embarrassed way.

"Do you want a lift?" I said, pointing to the car.

Joey Hooper looked up at the solid, stationary traffic and laughed.

"I won't have a lift, but I'll have a sit down. How about that?"

I smiled and we both got into the car. Joey sat with his rucksack on his lap and I looked round at his profile. When I'd known him his hair had been very short and he'd had the letter "H" sculpted into the side. It had given him a hard, mean look. He'd also carried a flick-knife round in his pocket.

"What happened to your hair?" I said.

He put his hand up to the place where the "H" used to be.

"They didn't have those kind of barbers in the nick, Patsy."

"No, course not," I said, feeling foolish.

"Hey, nice wheels!" he said, running his finger along the dashboard.

"Billy got it for me," I said proudly.

"How is he?"

Joey pulled a can of Coke out of his rucksack. He offered it to me but I shook my head.

"He's in Africa. It's a long story…" I said.

"Tell me," he said, pointing to the solid traffic. "I've got the time."

I told Joey the details about Billy's new job. Joey nodded and asked the right questions, how it came about, what made him want to do it, et cetera. Joey was a good listener, a person who was genuinely interested in other people. Somehow I ended up telling him a lot more than I'd intended to, my own feelings about Billy's decision, the reasons that I hadn't gone. And all the while I felt this feeling of regret surfacing slowly. I tutted at myself. Sitting in the middle of the London traffic with someone I hadn't seen for a while was not a good time to get emotional.

"That's enough about me," I said, noticing stirrings of movement from up ahead out the corner of my eye. "How are you?"

He shrugged his shoulders and hugged his rucksack.

"Tell me about prison, Joey. Go on, say the word. It won't bite you."

He gave me this sly smile and nodded his head.

"Hey, prison. It's what you'd expect. You keep your head down and don't upset anybody. You know what I'm saying?"

I nodded. Except that I didn't really know what he was saying.

"Listen Patsy. Prison was nothing for me. After

47

Paul died my family had a lot more grief to deal with than me being away for a few months."

I was quiet for a minute. The loss of a son or daughter or brother. It left a gaping hole in any family. I was reminded for a second of Kelly Ford's mother at the funeral, walking up the church aisle with Raymond tightly on her arm.

I reached across and put my hand on Joey's shoulder.

"Joey, we were so sorry, Billy and me, when Paul died. It wasn't right..."

"Nah. It wasn't right," Joey said.

A "bip" from behind made me jump and I looked ahead to see the traffic uncurling itself and moving slowly on. I turned the ignition on and moved ahead. For a couple of minutes the car was quiet.

"Are you working?" I said, in a light voice.

"Nope. I'm going to college in September. That's after resitting my A levels in June. I did some studying for them inside and my mum's paying for a couple of tutors. I should do all right."

The traffic was moving slowly forward and I could see the signs for road-works up ahead. I groaned inwardly. It was going to take for ever to get to the police station.

Joey reached over and picked up the padded envelope that was on the dashboard. He read out the name and address that was on the front.

"Still working as a detective?" he said.

"Yes," I said, "Although this isn't a case I'm actually working on, just something I've become involved in. Some kid was pushed off the top of Huxley Point. You might have read about it in the local paper?"

"Kelly Ford," Joey said.

"Yes," I said.

I wasn't surprised that Joey knew about it. It wasn't the sort of thing that happened every day. The newspapers and TV channels had been full of it.

"I'm just dropping something off at the local station," I went on, "then I can give you a lift home."

"I was in prison with her bloke. Vince Black," Joey said.

"Vincent Black? You were in the same prison? You knew him?" I said, surprised.

"We weren't exactly best friends, but I was on the right side of him and his mates."

"Oh."

"Very bad-tempered kid. Always blowing up at people. I was there on the day he attacked the girl-friend in the visiting room."

"You were?"

In that moment I had this strange, uncomfortable feeling about the case. I had stayed out of it right from the beginning, yet it seemed to be holding on to me. Every time I turned away from it, tried to push it away, something else came up and pulled me back in. It was as if I was *meant* to be involved in it.

Joey had continued talking.

"So I was facing him. One minute him and the girl were sitting talking, the next he made this grab for her throat. These screws came leaping across and dragged him out screaming. It was a bad business."

"Apparently he made threats to her," I said, pulling myself together.

"And then she sails off the edge of a building. Very neat. At least he's got the perfect alibi for not doing it himself."

"I don't suppose you ever heard him talk about someone called Liam Casey?"

"Vince's best mate? He spent most of his time going on about him."

The two traffic lanes were merging into one. Several large men in orange helmets were digging up the inside lane with a pneumatic drill that seemed to be in the car with us. Joey raised his voice.

"According to Vince, Liam would do anything he asked him to do. When they were ten Vince asked Liam to cut off his little finger and he did it! Course he spent a couple of days in hospital and had to have surgery. Still, Vince thought it was a laugh."

"No!" I said, curling my own fingers up.

"Mad guy, Vince was. Not too many brains."

"Did you talk to him much?" I said, finally moving past the end of the roadworks.

"Talk? You mean like this?" Joey shook his head.

"In prison blokes don't talk. I nodded to him when he passed me. I played cards with him half a dozen times. I chatted to him in the education wing. That was it."

We were coming up to the turning for the police station. I put my indicator on and was about to ask Joey about his family when he put his hand on my arm.

"Patsy, drop me off here will you? I don't feel like going anywhere near the Law."

"Right," I said, pulling into the side of the road and enduring the beeping of an irate driver who was behind me. Joey was rummaging in his rucksack. He pulled out a small black book and a pen and started to write.

"This is my mobile number."

"Thanks," I said, taking the piece of paper.

"Give me a ring. We could go out, see a film or something, have a drink."

"All right," I said, looking at the number that was scribbled on the page.

"Great to see you again," he said and squeezed my arm gently before getting out of the car.

I watched him walk away, his head tilting back to drink the Coke, his rucksack dangling loosely from one shoulder. Just up the street a policeman was getting out of a patrol car and Joey stopped, stepped off the curb and went across the road. It looked like he didn't even want to pass by him.

I folded up the piece of paper, shoved it into my jeans pocket and drove off.

The police station was full to bursting. I was behind two women who were complaining that their car had been towed away illegally and a young boy who kept walking up and down the small waiting area, staring menacingly at anyone who caught his eye.

"I just need to see Detective Inspector Warren," I said, when I finally got the Desk Sergeant's attention.

"Regarding what?" he said, not even looking at me.

"Some evidence I have for her. If you phone up and tell her I'm here I know she'll want to speak to me."

There was more than a hint of exasperation in my voice. The Desk Sergeant continued writing on a form that was in front of him and eventually spoke.

"I don't believe Detective Inspector Warren is in the building at the moment."

Just then I saw Des Murray coming out of the inside door.

"Des!" I raised my voice and he looked at me without expression.

Des Murray picked up a piece of paper from the desk and stood reading it, ignoring my call. He took his time, giving a couple of theatrical coughs, and then laid the paper back down where it came from. Then he walked in my direction.

"Do you know when Heather will be back? It's about the Kelly Ford case," I said, breathlessly.

He put his hand up to stop me speaking. As if he were a traffic policeman and I was an oncoming car.

"Look Miss Kelly, you've been told time and time again to keep out of police business. I know for a fact that Inspector Warren has instructed you to stay out of this investigation. Now if I was in your shoes I'd do what she says."

He put his hand down, confident no doubt that I wasn't about to run him over.

"Be a good girl and leave the police work to the big boys."

I found myself squeezing tightly on the padded envelope that I was holding. I wanted to say something really cutting, to put him in his place. But nothing came and I stood as still as a statue while he and the Desk Sergeant eyed each other wearily.

I plonked the padded envelope on the desk, turned with as much pride as I could muster, and left the building.

7

The Videos

The next morning, as I was about to leave for work, the phone rang. I picked up the receiver and said the number.

"Patsy, it's me, Heather."

"I was going to come and see you…" I started to say.

"I'm in the London Hospital. Can you come right now?"

"Are you all right? Have you been in an accident?"

"I've had a miscarriage, Patsy. Only I don't want anyone from work to know. For goodness' sake don't say anything to Tony. Can you come now? I'm in Sunflower Ward."

"I'll be about twenty minutes," I said and hung up.

*   *   *

It took me a little longer because I stopped off for some flowers, spring water and grapes. When I walked into Sunflower Ward I asked a nurse and she directed me to a small side ward where there were four beds. It was quiet and homely and somewhere in the background was a radio playing pop music. In a corner by the window was Heather. She was lying on her back staring up at the ceiling. When she saw me she leaned up on one elbow and attempted a smile of sorts. Her face was waxy though, and her eyes puffy, as though she'd been crying for a long time.

"How are you?" I said, holding out the flowers.

She nodded her head curtly as if to say *I'm bearing up, I'm OK*. But then after a couple of awkward seconds she began to shake her head and her face crumpled.

"Oh Heather," I said, embarrassed. I'd never seen her like this.

"I'm sorry," she spluttered, her eyes glassy, "you haven't told anyone, have you?"

"No," I said, putting the flowers on the bedside cabinet and sitting on the very edge of the bed.

"I couldn't bear anyone at work to know about this."

I nodded my head, even though I didn't really understand. She'd had a miscarriage. Why should that be a secret?

"I brought you something to drink," I said, for something to say.

"And grapes," she said, pointing to the brown paper bag I was carrying.

She plucked a grape out but before she could eat it she seemed to dissolve into silent sobs, her chin trembling with emotion.

"Oh Heather," I said, reaching out for her hand and holding it tightly, "maybe it was for the best."

She nodded her head.

"I know it is. It wasn't as if I was pleased about the pregnancy. You know, I told you. It wouldn't have fitted into my job or my life. How would I have managed?"

I nodded, silently. In the distance, beyond the music playing and the murmur of conversation, I thought I could hear the cries of a baby.

"I'd even considered an abortion."

"You hadn't made up your mind."

"I know, but now I've had it made up for me." She said it dismally, pulling three or four tissues from a box on the side and wiping her eyes and nose.

"The thing is," she continued, sniffing, "yesterday I was looking for some face cream in Boots and I found myself in the baby aisle. I spent ages looking at all these tiny clothes hanging up and I thought *Why would it be so terrible to have a baby?*"

I didn't speak. I could feel Heather's grip on my hand getting tighter. From far away I could still hear the insistent cries of someone else's baby. I wished more than anything that it would shut up.

"I could take maternity leave, employ a nanny. Lots of people do it. It wouldn't have to mean that I'd lose my career."

"I know," I said.

"But then last night I got these awful pains. I knew then, in that minute, that it was all over. That there wasn't going to be any baby."

"I'm so sorry," I said.

The ward was suddenly very quiet, even the crying baby had stopped. Heather lay back and pushed her face into the pillow.

A while later, when Heather had become calm again, she rang the CID office to tell them why she wasn't there. I sat quietly while she told the Sergeant that she'd been called away on family business for a few days. She sounded serious but firm; a complete contrast to her emotional outbursts a few minutes earlier. When the phone call was over she became upset again.

"I don't know why I'm telling you all this!" she said in a distracted way.

I knew why. Heather was a loner. She had colleagues, people who looked up to her, other people who didn't like her. As far as I knew, though, she didn't have much of a life outside work. Who else could she tell? Everyone she mixed with had something to do with the police force.

She remembered suddenly that she had some

papers and videos in her flat to do with the Kelly Ford investigation. In a fluster she hunted through her bags and produced her front door keys. She asked me to go and collect them and deliver them to Des Murray at the station. It was the last thing I felt like doing, but I couldn't turn her down.

Then she lay back on the pillow and closed her eyes. I knew she wasn't asleep but I whispered *good-bye* anyway. She gave the briefest of nods and turned away. I walked out of the tiny ward not knowing whether I should have stayed longer or not.

It was a short drive to her flat and I got there just before lunch-time. I let myself in and found the place unexpectedly tidy. There was a half finished cup of coffee on the kitchen drainer, that was all. On the kitchen table was a Boots bag which I opened. A pair of baby's booties dropped out with a receipt for two pounds ninety-five.

I felt this weary, sad feeling. Heather had just decided that she wanted her baby, then lost it. It was a funny phrase, *she lost her baby*, as though she'd put it somewhere and couldn't find it.

I went across to her desk and pulled together the things she'd told me to get. In her top drawer were the two videos she'd mentioned. I saw the words *Black/Mackenzie assault October 1997*. The second was *Prison Visit Kelly Ford/Vincent Black*.

I stood for a minute holding the videos. I had this urge to watch them. Call it curiosity. I wanted to see the faces of the people I'd been reading and hearing about. I wanted to see what had happened in that jeweller's shop.

Why not? Who was to know?

I sat down on a chair and slipped the first video into the player. On the label there were some numbers and I fast-forwarded the tape until I got to the right part. It was the inside of the jeweller's shop. The camera was obviously fixed on the ceiling looking down. The picture was surprisingly clear.

A woman was serving behind the counter, talking to a group of three young people, two girls and a boy. On the other side of the shop was a young man in his twenties standing waiting. Every now and then he looked at his watch. He was listening to a walkman, his head moving in time to some music. It had to be Dan Mackenzie, the young man who had ended up dead. I looked back to the group who were being served. One of the girls had bright red hair, but the other was blonde. I pressed the pause button and took a good look at Kelly Ford. She was thin and quite small. Her blonde hair was pulled back into a ponytail and she had bright lipstick on. She was wearing what looked like a black leather jacket with a zip up the front. I remembered I'd once had one just like it. I pressed the button again and the picture began to move. There was a lot of giggling going on and I could see the shop assistant getting annoyed. At one point she walked along the counter down to where Dan Mackenzie was and said something like, "I'll be with you in a minute, sir."

Carly Dickens noticed Mackenzie first. She looked round at him and then nudged Kelly. Kelly turned round, her eyes fixed on the waiting lad for a few seconds. It didn't look to me as though Mackenzie had even noticed the girls when Vince Black pulled Kelly roughly by the arm. Kelly stepped back and seemed to be laughing. Dan Mackenzie did look up then and I noticed him taking his earpiece out. The woman assistant was telling them to leave. Vince Black looked furious. He said something to Mackenzie. Then it looked as though Vince was throwing his head back to look at the ceiling, but without warning he headbutted the other lad.

I felt myself flinch and my teeth closed together.

Dan Mackenzie staggered back for a moment then lunged towards Vince Black. Somehow or other the young man seemed to trip and ended up on the floor, out of range of the camera. That's when Vince Black began to kick him. I found myself looking away, avoiding what was happening, and I caught sight of the shop assistant who was screaming, her mouth opening and shutting. Then my eye caught the two girls, Carly Dickens and Kelly Ford. Their faces had the strangest look. It was a mixture of fear and awe; as if they were scared but *impressed*.

Then it was all over. Vince and the two girls ran out

and after a few seconds the woman came out from behind the counter and bent down to where I assumed Dan Mackenzie was lying. A man entered from the back of the shop and there was a few minutes of milling around, then finally Dan Mackenzie staggered up, and I could see him fending off the woman and the man who were trying to keep him in the shop.

Then he left.

I stopped the video and looked at the second tape that was in my hand. On it were the words, *Property of HMP Pentonville*. I put it into the machine and fast-forwarded to the numbers marked on the box. Again the video camera was on the ceiling, and it showed a room with about a dozen tables and a number of civilians and prisoners sitting round talking. Dotted here and there were guards.

I felt the back of my neck tingle. It hadn't been that long ago that my boyfriend, Billy, had been accused of a crime he hadn't committed, and I'd visited him in a place that was very similar. It had been a miserable experience and I had come away with the smell of boiled vegetables and tobacco clinging to my hair.

I saw Vince Black facing the camera and a blonde-haired girl with her back to me. They were talking, then out of the blue Vince stood up and leaned across the table, grabbing Kelly by her hair. Everyone around stopped what they were doing and looked, and in no time two prison guards were behind Vince, pulling him, kicking and screaming, away from the frightened girl.

I ejected the tape and put it together with the other one into a box file that was on Heather's desk.

The box file was full of stuff about the case. I let my fingers rifle through it until I came to a see-through plastic wallet with half a dozen or so photographs of Kelly Ford. They were all the same, head and shoulder shots. They looked like they'd been cropped from a larger group photograph, probably for use in door to door inquiries, *Excuse me, sir, did you see this girl on May 1st?*

I took one out. It was the first time I'd had a good look at the girl who had asked for my help. She had blonde jaw-length hair and a thin face. She had striking blue eyes that were looking straight at the camera without a hint of a smile. From below her hair I could see the ends of some hoop earrings. They looked like curtain rings.

It was strange sitting looking at a girl I had never met and who was now dead. I hadn't known this girl when she was alive but since she'd died I'd heard a cassette tape of her voice, I'd seen her on video film and I'd looked closely into her face. I knew a lot about her and what she'd been doing for the last months of her life. The truth was I felt as though I did know her *personally*, and yet if she had lived she would be a stranger to me.

I decided that I wanted to keep the photograph.

Don't ask me why. I put it in my bag and closed up the box file. Then I looked around to make sure I hadn't left anything behind, and left.

At the police station I had intended just to leave everything with the Desk Sergeant. Unfortunately, I walked into the reception area just as Des Murray was walking out. I told him why I was there and he beckoned for me to follow him back into the offices.

"Where exactly is Inspector Warren?" he said with a sigh, as though he'd been searching everywhere for her. I handed him the box file. On the outside were the words *Kelly Ford Case*.

"She won't be in for a few days, she's got some family business to sort out."

"Has she now?" he said.

"She'll be back in a few days. I expect you can cope till then."

"Oh, we will," Des Murray said.

He dumped the box file on a desk without looking at it. I looked across at the whiteboard and was dismayed to see a map of the immediate area drawn on it. At the top were the words, *Vandalism – Zero Tolerance*.

"What happened to the Kelly Ford investigation?" I said.

"On the back burner, Miss Kelly," Des Murray said, opening a newspaper.

"You're not following it up any more?" I asked.

"I didn't say that. Any leads develop and we'll follow them up. But life goes on. Crime in the East End doesn't stop because of the murder, or suicide, of one sixteen–year–old girl."

"Suicide? I thought you'd discounted that?"

"We're keeping an open mind. Nothing is ever black and white, Miss Kelly. Now if you don't mind we've got a job to do. We must keep the place ship-shape until Inspector Warren returns."

He manoeuvred me through door of the CID room and into the reception area. A moment later I found myself standing on the other side of the desk watching Des Murray's back disappear behind the door. The Desk Sergeant gave me an impatient stare and I turned and left the station.

8

Carly Dickens

When I got home I went up to my bedroom and took a good long look in the mirror. I wasn't pleased with what I saw. My skin looked blotchy and flushed. My hair was sticking out untidily and even my glasses were smeared. I honestly couldn't remember when I had last given them a good soapy wash.

My clothes weren't much better. I'd been wearing the same pair of jeans for days and my T-shirt hadn't even been ironed.

I must have looked like a real layabout when I was at the police station. No wonder they treated me like a kid. I sat down on the bed and pulled the duvet up around me. I should take more care with my appearance. Just because Billy had gone abroad it didn't mean I had to let myself go.

I felt disgruntled with these thoughts, as though I wasn't really getting to the heart of the matter. I tried to imagine Billy being there at that moment and even then I couldn't really muster up much enthusiasm for getting showered and dressed up. Then there was Joey Hooper. He was a friend. Somewhere in my pocket I had his phone number. I could ring him up, arrange to go out.

Even this didn't make me feel any better.

I picked up my bag and pulled out the photograph of Kelly Ford. I looked at it for a minute. This girl had contacted me because she had been afraid. I'd put her letter to one side then someone had killed her. That was something I deeply regretted. Since then I'd been told to back off.

I'd tried. I'd deliberately kept away and left the police to do their job.

But everywhere I turned the case came back at me. Raymond Ford had come to see me; Joey Hooper had known Vince Black; I had watched as Dan Mackenzie fought his last fight. All the time I'd been avoiding being drawn in.

But I was involved. I was at the heart of it. I always had been.

It was why I was feeling disgruntled and lethargic. The case had been mine from the beginning but I'd let go of it and watched it from a distance. It had made me feel frustrated and useless. That's why I'd lost interest in everything, including myself.

The decision to get involved, to follow up the case, only took a second. It was like a door I was opening. On the other side was everything that was important – Kelly's murder and my need to be part of it. I'd been contacted by her; I'd been to her funeral; now I was going to be part of catching her murderer.

It felt right, and out of nowhere there was a buzz of energy in my feet, in my hands. I stood up, went downstairs and took the phone book off the hallstand.

There were nine numbers for *Dickens* in the area book. I had no choice but to ring each one and ask if Carly Dickens was at home. On the fourth phone call I hit lucky.

"Is Carly in?" I said brightly, trying to sound like a close friend.

"Nah, she's at work," a female voice said.

"Oh right, I thought she might be," I said, as though I'd expected it. "I'll ring her at work. Is she still at that place … where was it now?"

"McDonald's," the woman said, "at Stratford. Only they won't like you ringing her when she's working. She gets off about ten. You could ring her then."

"Oh thanks, I will."

I put the phone down and looked in the hall mirror. I saw myself smiling. It was a small start.

* * *

At ten o'clock I sat in my car across the street from McDonald's. It had started to rain and every few seconds the windscreen became blurred, so I clicked the wipers on and off and looked across at the entrance of the restaurant. The car was silent and warm and from inside I could hear the traffic splashing past, and see tiny darts of rain in other people's headlights.

Carly Dickens came out about five-past-ten. She stood still for a few minutes fiddling with an umbrella. The lights from the restaurant spilled out into the street and I could see her clearly. Her red hair was jaw-length and stood out from her face. She had on a zip-up jacket, jeans and boots. Even though she was dressed casually her height made her look elegant.

I got out of the car and walked towards her.

"Excuse me," I said, pulling my collar up to keep the rain out.

She didn't speak. She just looked puzzled.

"My name is Patsy Kelly and your friend Kelly wrote to me a few days before she was killed. I wonder, if it's not too much trouble, could I talk to you about her? Ask you a few questions?"

Her face showed no expression but she looked closely at me.

"It's just that I'd like to know a bit about her. For my own peace of mind."

"Why don't you ask her family?" she said.

"You were her friend. If anyone knew her well it was you," I said, hoping to win her over.

"I'm on my way home."

"I could give you a lift," I said, turning to point at my car. "It's just a few questions, that's all."

She looked at the car and then at me. Just then a gust of wind swept the rain in our direction and she had to hold her umbrella at a defensive angle. My glasses were speckled with drops and I was beginning to shiver.

"Hey, why not," she said, throwing the words in my direction, "at least it'll keep me dry."

We got into the car in silence. I took my glasses off and rubbed them against my jeans.

"Where do you live?" I said.

"Forest Gate, near Wanstead Flats," she said, "I usually get the train."

"I know how to get there," I said, moving out into the traffic.

"I'd heard that Kelly contacted someone," she said after a while, "I had no idea she was so scared."

"You hadn't seen her for a while?" I said, squinting my eyes to avoid some bright headlights that were behind me.

"Not since she last went to see my cousin Vince in prison. She avoided me. I knew she'd finished with him. I was hacked off with her."

"She said that after Vince killed Dan Mackenzie she was afraid of him."

"Don't believe it for a minute. Kelly was all over him that day. Then when he got sent down after Mackenzie died she didn't want to know him any more!"

I said nothing while we drove through the traffic. The rain was coming down a little heavier and I concentrated on where I was going. Carly kept talking. "The fact is that Kelly wanted Vince when times were good. Once Vince got put away she cooled off. But that was Kelly. One minute she wanted one thing and the next she wanted something else. Look, don't think I'm being rude, but why are you asking me this stuff? I thought the police were investigating it."

"Raymond Kelly came to see me. He has a cassette tape on which Kelly says that she's scared of Vince. Raymond mentioned Liam Casey's name to me. He says that Liam is Vince's best mate and would do anything for him."

"It's ridiculous. Sure, Vince got angry at Kelly. Sure, he threatened her. But he didn't mean it!"

"What about Liam Casey, though? Might he have had something to do with her death? Weren't you seeing him? You knew him quite well," I said, pulling her back to Liam.

"I'm not exactly on speaking terms with him. We broke up months ago."

She was quiet for a minute and I noticed signs for Forest Gate. I began to panic. I'd be dropping her off in a minute and I hadn't said all I wanted. I slowed down.

"Wait a minute," she said suddenly, her voice louder, "is Raymond Ford going round trying to stir up trouble? He's sent you to see me hasn't he? He wants me to grass Liam up."

"No, he just wants to find out the truth," I said.

"If anyone should be asked about Kelly's death it should be soft Raymond. He had a sort of, what do you call it, *thing* about his sister."

"What do you mean?"

"Like an ... what's that word? An *obsession*. That's it. They grew up really close. Until a couple of years ago when Kelly started seeing people. Raymond didn't like it. He used to hang around the places that she went. Hey, he didn't even like me being her friend. He was really nasty to me. He wanted her all to himself."

"Her own brother?"

"It was weird. Sometimes Kelly liked it, you know, an older brother watching over her. Mostly she was hacked off with it. Vince even threatened him once, told him to get lost. Here, take the second on the left after this pub. My street's the first on the right. Be careful with the roadworks."

I slowed down before the turning and put my indicator on.

"Why was Mrs Ford so unpleasant to you?" I said. "At the funeral, I mean?"

"You don't want to take any notice of that. Maureen, Kelly's mum, she's got a real drink problem. She has bad mood swings. It used to upset Kelly. I know Maureen blamed me for introducing Kelly to Vince."

I turned left and found myself driving along the edge of open forest. It wasn't so much a road as a lane, thin and long.

"Here, pull in and I'll walk from here. My house is just up the road."

There was no pavement so I tucked in beside a tree.

"Can you give me Liam's phone number? Or address? I'd really like to talk to him."

"Liam moved months ago. I don't know where he lives. He rings me now and then. He's no angel." She laughed. "I know more about Liam than most people, stuff that would get him into trouble if anyone knew. But he wouldn't kill anyone."

I opened my mouth to speak but Carly Dickens had already taken her seat-belt off and opened the passenger door.

"Thanks for the lift. I live further up and it's a dead end. You need to turn round here."

"OK," I said, glumly.

A three point turn in a dark lane on a wet night in an area that I didn't know. It was all I needed.

"You want to ask someone about Kelly's death, you go back and ask Raymond. He's not as soft as he looks."

The door closed behind her and I sat back feeling disconcerted. The indicator was still winking on and off and the wipers were swinging back and forth. I turned the ignition key and everything came to a stop. There was only the sound of the rain on the roof of the car.

Carly Dickens had put her umbrella up and was walking up the middle of the roadway. The only streetlights were on the other side, away from the forest. Ahead of me were the back lights of a hatch-back that was parked. Like me, it was stationary, the driver sitting, staring straight ahead.

I watched as Carly moved around it further out into the road, her long legs taking confident strides along the dark tarmac. I was reminded of the time when she swaggered into the church, late for Kelly's funeral, and her sudden tears as she saw Kelly's mum. How genuine was she? She certainly didn't seem to have much regard for her dead friend.

I sighed and decided that I should go. I turned the ignition key and put my indicator on. Up in front I could still see Kelly, getting further away, her head tucked under her umbrella. I turned the steering wheel sharply to the right and opened my window to check for traffic.

I was just about to move off, when the driver in front moved out without warning. In fact he had no lights on at all. I flashed my headlights to alert him but there was no response and the car moved off up the road. I could just see Carly in the distance. I flashed my lights again, three or four times but the car seemed to speed up, revving away from where I was, disappearing into the dark. I sat for a minute, perplexed. Then from out of the black night I heard a screech of brakes that made my eardrums ring and my shoulderblades jump. I turned the ignition off and got out of the car, all the time squinting into the dark, through the rain, to see what had happened.

There'd been an accident, I knew.

In the distance I saw some white lights appear. They were only pin points at first but they got bigger as they came nearer. The hatchback was reversing down the street towards me. Further up, beyond it there were lights and voices and some sort of commotion. The driver had hit somebody. About six metres away from me the hatchback braked sharply. I took a few steps towards it but stopped as it did a frantic three point turn, and with a loud squeal of its wheels it roared past me down the narrow road.

It all happened so quickly. In the blink of an eye the car had turned out on to the main road and was gone.

Then I heard a voice from behind me and I turned to see a middle aged man half-running, half-walking towards me.

"Did you get the number?" he said, coming to a halt, his breath coming in great gasps.

"No, it was too fast…" I said, stupidly.

"That red car. It had no lights. It hit a girl."

I ran off up the lane and joined the gathering group of people who had come out of their houses because of the noise. Saying "*Excuse me, can you let me through*," I edged past people who were hugging themselves against the chilly night air and the rain. About thirty metres up I got to a small knot of people standing, looking down.

On the ground, lying on her side, was Carly Dickens. A man was squatting down by her, his finger on her neck. Someone else was kneeling down opening her mouth. There was blood on the road and on her clothes and her arm was at a very odd angle.

"There's a pulse," the man said.

"Thank God for that," I heard a woman from behind say.

A metre away, upended on the ground, was Carly's umbrella. I walked across and picked it up. Then I stood holding it over the injured girl on the ground, and waited for the ambulance.

9

Casualty

The ambulance swooped round the corner within minutes. The paramedics, a man and a woman, bounced out and ran to Carly's side. The man moved everyone back while the woman knelt down and listened to Carly's breathing. Within seconds she had attached a drip to the girl's arm and put a neck collar on her.

A couple of people asked tentative questions. "*Is she all right?*" "*Is she badly injured?*" The paramedics said nothing though. When she disappeared into the ambulance, the woman turned and said something like, "*It's too soon to say, we're doing the best we can.*" Her face was stony.

I walked around in a numb state. There were a couple of other onlookers who were upset and crying. They were being comforted by some of the householders who had come out and witnessed the aftermath of the accident.

A woman who had been walking her dog had actually seen it.

"I had Tilly off the lead and the car just came out of the darkness. It was going really fast and it had no lights. I couldn't see much, but it was red. I remember that. It was a red car."

The police arrived sometime around then and took our details, and then told us to go home. I was grateful to get away. I got straight back into my car, did a three point turn of my own and drove off.

I drove out of Carly's road and found myself in a state of confusion about where to go. I followed a signpost to Stratford. As I left the accident site behind me I felt this weak, fluttery feeling inside. I pulled over to the side of the road and sat for a few minutes taking deep breaths.

A *red* car. I sat very still, feeling the traffic pass by me on the dark road. The rain was falling at an angle, skidding across the windscreen, distorting the lights of oncoming cars. The car that hit Carly Dickens had been red. Kelly Ford had said that it was a red car that she thought had been following her. A *red car* that she had seen parked in her street.

It had been a hit-and-run. That's what people had said. The driver had made frantic attempts to get away afterwards. Could it have been a terrible accident? The driver, shocked at what he had done, speeding away out of panic?

I wasn't sure. How could I be? I needed to talk to someone about it. There were things that needed to be sorted out, cleared up. I wanted Billy beside me saying, *Look Patsy, it was dark; the guy probably didn't realize his lights were off. She's walking along the middle of the road. He doesn't see her till the last minute when it's already too late.*

But the passenger's seat was empty. I was sitting by myself, parked on the edge of the road with the rain slicing across the windscreen and cars screaming past me. I felt painfully alone.

When I got home my head was heavy and my neck was rigid with tension. I walked straight into the living room hoping to pull my mum out of the arms of Gerry and into the kitchen for a conversation. I didn't usually bother her with my work because she worried so much. But she was bright and level-headed and I couldn't think of anyone else I could call on.

The living room was full of people though.

"Patsy, here come and meet some of my colleagues. Look everyone, here's my clever daughter."

Half a dozen faces looked around at me. They were smiling and I noticed a number of crystal wine glasses twinkling under the light. On the floor were several wrapped-up wedding presents, and up on the ceiling were a number of helium balloons with the words *You're getting married!* on them. My mum was smiling broadly, her relaxed expression suggesting that she'd had several glasses of wine herself.

I remembered then that she'd invited her work friends that evening. She'd mentioned it earlier but it had gone out of my mind.

"Hello," I said with a forced smile.

"Here, have some wine," a voice said and a glass was produced magically.

"No, actually, I won't if you don't mind. I…"

They were all looking at me, their eyes slightly glazed. I knew that I should take the wine, join in the festivities, leave the accident business until later. It was my mum's wedding after all. I shouldn't be the one to put a damper on it.

I couldn't though. The thought of settling down amid the gaiety and the jokes and the drinks was more than I could bear. I needed quiet, I needed to be alone.

"I'm just too tired," I said, "I need an early night."

They all looked a bit unsure and Gerry got up and put his arm loosely round my shoulder.

"All right Pats. You get your beauty sleep. We'll have a drink for you."

There was a mild giggle at that and people started to talk again. I left the room and was about to go upstairs when my mum's anxious face appeared.

"Is everything all right?" she said, holding her wine glass at a dangerous angle.

"Fine, I'm just really tired."

Her eyes creased up at the corners and she looked like she wasn't going to let it go. A burst of laughter came from behind her though and she was drawn back into the living room.

I went upstairs, got undressed and went to bed.

I lay there in the dark listening to the sounds from below. My mum's friends were laughing and talking, and after a while there was the sound of music and voices singing, some of them loud and boisterous.

I made myself think of the dark lane and the policeman squatting down to look at the skid marks on the road, writing things down on a notepad, shaking his head at his own thoughts. The other officer was intermittently speaking into a small hand-held radio. He'd taken the names and addresses of the people there. We might be called on to make statements, he'd said. I felt a mild panic thinking of this. When Des Murray found out that I had driven Carly I would be in trouble for interfering.

I let this thought worry me for a while before I eventually fell into a light sleep. When I woke up the clock said 2.23.

The house was completely silent and all I could hear was the patter of the rain on the windows. I sat up and turned my bedside light on. The sleep had taken the edge off my tiredness and I made myself go back to the beginning, when I had been waiting outside McDonald's.

I hadn't warmed to Carly Dickens at all. She'd been Kelly's closest friend, and yet she hadn't shown any signs of grief. She hadn't got on with Kelly's mother or brother; she'd fallen out with her boyfriend Liam, and in the end she'd stopped seeing Kelly herself. She made a spirited defence of Vincent Black, who had killed someone. At no time had she spoken affectionately about her dead friend.

And now she'd been deliberately run over.

I leaned over to retrieve my rucksack from the floor where I'd dumped it earlier. I pulled out my notepad. The facts of the case were buzzing irritatingly round my head and I wanted to pin them down. I began to write about the case, as though it was a kind of story. I started with the words, *Someone pushed Kelly Ford off the top of Huxley Point on the 1st May.* I continued writing for a long time. The only sound in the room was the rain and the crinkle of a page turning over. I described the letter that was sent to me, the visit I had had from Raymond Ford, the cassette tape, and the conversation I'd had with Carly Dickens before she'd been knocked down. I added the stuff about my visit to Heather's flat and the video footage of Dan Mackenzie, and of Vincent Black, Kelly and Carly.

I sat up straight and flicked through the pages I'd written. It was 3.48. I'd been writing for over an hour. I felt good. It was as if I'd reduced the uncertainties of the case to a half a dozen pages of neatish handwriting.

Two girls; one dead and the other injured. The link was the red car.

I sat back. I knew I should phone Des Murray then and there and either tell him or leave a message about the presence of the red car. He would sneer though, and tell me yet again to keep out of it. I couldn't do that any more.

Then I looked back at the beginning of my story. Kelly Ford was pushed off Huxley Point. Why Huxley Point? Was it significant in some way? Did the killer live there, or near there? Was it a place that Kelly and Vince had visited? I knew from past experience that the places in which people are murdered are usually important in some way either to the killer or the person who has been killed.

At the bottom of my page I wrote the words *WHY HUXLEY POINT?* in capital letters and sat back. I ought to start at the beginning, I thought, where the murder took place. Then I lay back feeling contented, and must have drifted off to sleep.

I woke up early and had a long shower. Then I pulled a long skirt and T-shirt out of my wardrobe. I added a woolly cardigan for warmth. I stood on tiptoe to look at the collection of hats that I keep on top of my wardrobe. I shook my head. I wasn't in a hat mood. I put some make-up on, a little mascara and some lipstick, and took my stuff downstairs.

My mum and Gerry were still asleep, so I was on my own. I made myself some breakfast and used the kitchen table as a place to sort out my papers from the case. I made a neat pile and then got the stapler from my mum's desk and clipped them together.

On the top was a loose sheet with a name and phone number scribbled on it.

I walked out to the hall with my toast in my hand and made three phone calls. One was to the office answerphone where I left a message for my uncle Tony.

The second call was to the London Hospital to see how Carly Dickens was. I gave my name and said that I was her cousin.

"*Carly Dickens is in a serious but stable condition,*" the voice said, "*I'm afraid that's all the information I can give you.*"

It was all the information that I needed. Carly Dickens was still alive. That was the important thing.

The third phone call I made was to Joey Hooper.

I picked him up at his house in Highbury a couple of hours later.

"All right Patsy?" he said, grinning. "Where we going?"

"We're going to look at the place where Kelly Ford died."

"The tower block. Suits me. OK Sherlock, let's get going."

I felt this stab of sadness even though Joey was trying to cheer me up. *Sherlock Holmes*; it was a nickname that Billy had used when I first started the job. In the couple of years that I'd been working as a detective Billy had helped me more than anyone. He had been my driver, my assistant, my confidant. More than anything he had acted as the voice of reason when a case had got out of hand. I hadn't always taken his advice, but I'd been grateful for it. Now Billy was gone and Joey was sitting in his place. Had I just replaced him?

"Have I said something wrong?" Joey said.

"No," I said, forcing a smile, "I haven't slept much, that's all."

Feeling a little uneasy, I put my indicator on and pulled out into the traffic.

10
Huxley Point

The tower block was close to Stratford. It sat on the edge of an estate that was undergoing radical changes. It had been built along with three other identical blocks in the nineteen-seventies. At that time they were thought to be the answer to everyone's prayers. Homes in the sky, smart new apartments with lifts and panoramic views of the East End.

Now there was only one tower block left. The other three had been demolished, making way for new low-rise council houses. Huxley Point was destined for the same fate.

I'd got all this information from a local newspaper report headlined *Death in a Dead End Estate*.

We saw it looming up from a fair distance away,

standing its ground and out of place like some startled dinosaur. The area around it looked bleak; empty housing, shops with their shutters up, kids hanging round even though it was in school hours.

I parked the car and turned the engine off.

Around the tower block was a stretch of grassland about the size of a football field. There were some empty flower beds and an overgrown shrub garden that was doubling as a rubbish dump. A couple of cars were abandoned on different bits of the grass, one burnt out and the other with no wheels and the words *WEST HAM RULES* painted across the windscreen.

I got out of the car and locked it firmly, hoping it would be there when I returned. I found myself looking upwards at the top of the building, my eye running up and down the distance between the roof and the ground.

"Just tell me again what it is we're going to do here?" Joey said, his hands deep in his pockets, his shoulders hunched.

I could see he wasn't comfortable being back in the East End. He'd lived here until he was a teenager, but his family had suffered a lot of racial abuse, and moved to Highbury. It was hard enough me coming to a place where I wasn't known, where people might be looking round the edge of their net curtains at a strange face on the estate. But for a black kid whose brother had been killed by racists it was probably nerve-racking. I took his arm and we walked towards the entrance.

"I just want to get a feel of the place, that's all. The police said that most of the flats are empty. I'm thinking we might see some residents who could have remembered something, who'll feel comfortable talking to me when they didn't talk to the police."

"Oh, that's all," Joey said, smiling widely. "You're just hoping that by coming here we can solve the case!"

"Exactly!" I said, jokingly.

Huxley Point had one of those phone entry systems that had long ago stopped working. The doors were swinging open and we walked into the foyer to an overwhelming smell. I can't say exactly what it was. There was a scent of cooking and general stuffiness but mostly it was the smell of decay; of a place where people had stopped bothering, of a building that was slowly crumbling.

Joey and I took the lift. It was sitting on the ground floor, the doors partially closed in front of us. Inside it was tatty, but the lights were on and it seemed to be working. The only other choice was to walk up sixteen storeys.

"Why don't we go right to the top and work our way down? See if any of the upper flats are occupied," Joey said.

"Heather said they were empty."

"Officially, yeah. You might find some people squatting though. A building like this. It'll have water and mains electricity. Anyone good with a screwdriver could make a place liveable."

It was a good point. I'd had contacts with homeless people in the past and I knew that they squatted wherever they could. I pressed the button and the lift began to move slowly up. Joey kept talking.

"Sixteen storeys. Probably four flats on each floor. That makes sixty-four flats."

"Over half of them are probably empty," I said.

"So if we work our way down we could knock at each occupied flat, talk about the day of the murder."

"What if they ask who we are?" I said, my forehead wrinkling.

"We'll say we're Kelly's friends. In a way it's true."

"I suppose so," I said.

He was right. It was a fair thing to say.

The lift started to slow down and came to a shuddering stop at the sixteenth floor. We walked out on to a landing that was mostly in shadow. The ceiling lighting wasn't working. The only light was from outside and it shone in through four strips of window. It was quiet as well, the noise from the traffic from far below only just audible. It gave the place a church-like feel. We could see what used to be four front doors, each now covered with a sheet of perforated metal.

It was a depressing place, the walls scarred with graffiti, the plaster lifting from the damp. Even the metal doors looked second-hand, scuffed, their paint peeling, small holes appearing where the metal had given way. We walked up to one and Joey lifted up a heavy padlock that had the word CHUBB stamped on it in big block letters. He went round to each of them in turn checking that they were locked up.

"Look over there," I said, pointing to a set of stairs in the corner.

"The entrance to the roof."

We walked across and stood at the bottom of a flight of stairs leading up to what looked like a brand new metal door. It was heavy and solid and had a Chubb lock at the top and bottom. A new notice on it said *STRICTLY FORBIDDEN*. The phrase *closing the stable door after the horse has bolted* came into my mind. Over the metal banister were the remains of a strip of police incident tape. It hung limply in the semi-darkness, hardly visible at all.

"No chance of anyone getting out on the roof again," Joey said.

"Nope."

Heather said the old roof door had been hanging open. Had the door, like the rest of the flats, been falling apart?

We walked out into the stairwell. One side of it was glass and looked out on the surrounding area. It was quite a view. A grey cat emerged from behind an old chair that had been dumped in the corner. It walked towards us, meowing hungrily.

"Careful," Joey said. "It might be wild."

I squatted down and looked at it warily. Its coat was sleek and its eyes were clean and bright.

"It probably lives with one of the tenants," I said, "I wonder what it's doing up here."

"Exploring?" Joey said, giving it a pat on the head.

We left it there and went down visiting each of the next seven floors. They were all deserted, the front doors covered with the same tatty metal mesh and heavy Chubb lock. The whole place was eerie, each landing was in heavy shadow with odd bits of rubbish lying like tumbleweed.

When we got to the eleventh floor it was cleaner, with a couple of doors that had no mesh. We knocked but found nobody at home.

"Squatters?" I said.

Joey shrugged his shoulders and we kept going down.

All the flats on the sixth floor were lived in. We knocked on three doors but there was no answer. A woman in a duffel coat emerged from the last one. She was young with very short white-blonde hair and a ring through her eyebrow.

"Excuse me," I said.

"If you're from the council, you're wasting your time," she said. She had a rucksack with her and looked as though she was going to a college.

"We're not," I said, walking along with her and standing as she pressed the lift button. "We're just trying to see if anyone remembers anything about the girl who was pushed off the roof a couple of weeks ago."

In my hand I held out the picture of Kelly.

"Are you from the police?" she said, with some aggression.

"No."

"Definitely not," Joey said. "We're Kelly's friends. We're just trying to sort things out." He put his arm loosely round my shoulder.

The girl looked at each of us in turn. She seemed to relax visibly.

"I didn't see anything until it was all over. It was a terrible thing. It really upset us."

"You saw her fall?"

"No, but I was in the flat when it happened. I heard the sirens and then I looked out of my window. I saw her lying there, on the ground. It was horrible."

"But you didn't see her come into the building or go up in the lift?"

She shook her head.

"Do you know anyone who might have seen her?"

"Nope. People mind their own business here. Since all the old tenants moved out it's used for short term lets; students, problem families, see? People here are always changing. They see a better place, they're out like a shot. New people come in, others move out. No one notices if someone strange walks up the stairs."

She pressed hard on the lift button again.

"I never saw the girl and I don't think anyone else did. But even if she had been seen I doubt anyone would have registered it."

I could hear the lift grumbling up.

"Thanks for your help," I said.

The lift doors opened and the girl went in.

"You're welcome," she said with a shrug. "Sorry I haven't got any information for you."

We walked wearily down the remaining flights of stairs noticing the build-up of black plastic rubbish bags and old bits of worn-out or broken furniture. All the landings were similar. A couple of people came to their doors and gave us curt answers or simply told us to clear off. As we got closer to the bottom there were more kids around. As I knocked on the doors I could see Joey chatting to them.

In the end though we reached the bottom no wiser than we'd been at the top. We walked outside and I was grateful for the blast of fresh air. I was also relieved to see my car still where I'd parked it.

"So basically someone could have brought Kelly

here, taken the lift or walked to the top without a soul noticing." I said, sitting on the low wall that cut off the shrub garden from the grass. A few metres behind me were the remains of an old telly that had been chucked there.

"Looks like it," Joey said, using his foot to fiddle with something that was on the ground.

"Whoever killed Kelly must have planned this. They must have known about this block. Maybe they lived in it at some time?"

"Could be," Joey said.

"Otherwise, how would they know that it was possible to get on to the roof?" Joey didn't speak, just shrugged his shoulders. He picked something up from the ground.

"Oh!" I said it with pretend temper. "How is it possible for a girl to go off the roof of a building in broad daylight and for nobody to see anything?"

"I've got it!" Joey said.

"You have?" I looked at him in surprise.

"No, no. Not about that. It's just something that's been niggling me. Look," he said, showing me something he'd picked up off the ground.

It was a padlock. A tiny one. The kind a kid would have for a school locker. I looked blankly at him.

"Follow me," he said, taking my hand and leading me back into the building.

He pressed the lift button and looked at me in an excited way.

"What?" I said.

But he put his finger over his lips and we were silent all the way back up to the top floor where we were met by the grey cat, still meowing fiercely.

"Look," Joey said, and walked over to one of the doors that was covered with the metal grille. He lifted the padlock. It was solid and heavy and I raised my shoulders questioningly.

"I was looking at this when you called me over to the roof door. All the other padlocks, every single one of them, have the word CHUBB on them. This one doesn't. Someone has opened this flat up and replaced the padlock with another one, so that at a glance it looks like it's not occupied."

"So?"

"So, someone lives here. Not just squatting. Someone lives here *in secret*."

The cat was waltzing through my feet, its tail licking at my legs. I stood for a minute letting Joey's words sink in.

"And another thing. They're still living here now. Look at this cat. It's well looked after and it needs to be fed. The person who lives here could show up any minute."

"How did the police miss this flat when they were doing door-to-door?"

"It was padlocked. It looks the same as the other flats on the landing. They assumed it was empty."

I looked at it for a minute and then lifted the

padlock up in my hand. It was different to the others. The area around it did look very scuffed, as though someone had been working away at it. There was even a small round hole in the mesh. I made a fist and put my hand through.

"See," Joey said excitedly, "when the tenant goes into the flat they pull the metal closed behind them, put their hand through, and close the padlock. Then they close the front door and it looks just the same as any of the other doors."

"But why go to all that trouble?" I said. "Plenty of people squat in places like this."

"Because they have something to hide?"

My face must have had a perplexed look because Joey continued. "Think about what you said downstairs. The person who killed Kelly must have known about this building and the way to the roof."

He looked at me, waiting for me to say something.

"The killer might live here?" I said, incredulous.

"Why not?" Joey said. "Think about what that girl said. People who live here don't take any notice of new faces."

"But that was about Kelly. You're talking about someone who lived here day in, day out! Honestly Joey, think logically. Someone must have seen them!"

I must have raised my voice because Joey stopped talking.

"I mean, it'd be too easy if the solution was as

simple as that. Believe me, murders are always more complicated. I know. I've been through a lot."

"OK, OK. You've made your point. But don't forget, I've been through a murder as well," Joey said, in a tiny, tight voice.

He was talking about his brother Paul. I clenched my fists in annoyance with myself. How could I have been so insensitive? Joey, more than anyone, knew about murder investigations. I tried my best to repair the situation.

"I'm sorry, Joey. I should think before I speak. There's no harm at all in trying to talk to the person or people who live here," I said, grudgingly.

But Joey had gone back over to the lift and pushed the button. He was put out. I put my hand on his sleeve and gave his arm a squeeze. The last thing I wanted to do was upset him.

"Let's come back later, say around teatime. Like you said, the cat needs feeding. Whoever lives here must be back by then."

Joey gave a little nod and a half-smile but he was quiet all the way down in the lift.

Sometimes I should just keep my big mouth shut.

11

Mothers and Sons

After I'd dropped Joey off I went back to the office. My uncle was out. On my desk there were some scribbled messages and phone numbers.

Where were you? Ring round overdue accounts. I'm in court the rest of the day. Tony.

Raymond Ford rang. Needs to speak to you.

Des Murray rang about a hit-and-run.

The hit-and-run. I felt a twinge of anxiety. At some point I would have to see Des Murray and tell him that I had driven Carly home, that I had been interviewing her about the Kelly Ford case. I wasn't looking forward to it.

The first thing I did was to ring Raymond Ford.

"Raymond's not in at the moment," a female voice said.

"Am I speaking to Mrs Ford?"

"Yes, but if you're a journalist I've got absolutely nothing to say." she started, her voice surprisingly nasty.

"Mrs Ford, I'm a friend of Raymond's. He rang me this morning. I was hoping to come round and see him."

"My Raymond rang you? Who are you? He didn't say."

"My name's Patsy."

"Come round. He'll be back any time now."

"Could you tell me what number you live at? I wrote it down but I seem to have mislaid the paper."

"We're at twenty-two Cooper's Road. It's about five minutes from Stratford tube station. Come any time, dear."

I scribbled the address on to a notepad and put the phone down. Then I packed up my stuff and put the list of messages back into my top drawer. I pulled the A-Z of London out of the drawer and stood up to leave.

It took just over ten minutes to walk from the station. I hadn't taken the car because I knew it would be impossible to park. It was one of a row of terraced houses that edged on to an older estate of three-storey flats. I rang the bell and a couple of moments later Mrs Ford answered the door.

She was smaller than I remembered her from the funeral. I'd expected her to be in black but she was

wearing blue leggings and a flowery top. She had a
very strong perfume on, as though she'd just
sprayed some on that minute. It wasn't unpleasant.
She was holding an unlit cigarette in one hand. In
the other she had a small gold lighter.

"Mrs Ford?" I started to say.

"Are you Patsy?" she said, stepping out on to the
path and looking up and down the street. "Don't
mind me. I'm just making sure there's no one around.
People round here are so nosy. Do come in."

She brushed against me and that was when I
noticed the faintest whiff of alcohol. It was hidden
underneath the heavy scent.

I followed her into the living room and sat myself
on an armchair. The room was light and airy and there
were flower prints everywhere; floral wallpaper and
curtains, and even the seat covers had big rose blooms.

"You'll have to excuse me, love. I have to be
careful of the press. They bothered us night and day
when my Kelly was first killed. Dreadful, it was."

"That's terrible," I said.

Mrs Ford closed her eyes and was shaking her
head. I waited, hoping that she wasn't going to get
upset. After a few seconds she seemed to pull
herself together and she started to speak.

"Can I get you a cup of tea?"

"No, thanks, I've just had one."

She clicked the lighter and held it up to her
cigarette. For a second she looked unsteady on her

feet. Then she was all right. I wondered how much she had had to drink. She gave me a quick smile and I looked away, embarrassed, wishing that Raymond would hurry up.

My eye caught a shelf above the TV. It was covered in small cactus plants, at least a dozen of them. Mrs Ford saw me looking.

"My Raymond collects those. Personally I don't like them much, but you know what kids are like. They're called succulents. Funny name, isn't it?"

It was a funny name. I looked at the odd-shaped little plants, their thorns sticking out spitefully against the softness of the floral wallpaper. I imagined them sucking moisture greedily from the air.

"I shouldn't call him a kid, should I? But you know they're always our babies, whatever age they are."

Her eyes glassed over suddenly and she used the back of her hand to wipe at them.

"I'm sorry, Mrs Ford, I should leave you alone," I said, standing up, not knowing what to say. It had been a bad idea to come.

"Please, don't worry yourself. The doctor says I must cry if I feel like it."

She walked across to the mirror over the mantelpiece and dabbed at her eyes with a tissue.

"Raymond tells me he was very close to his sister," I said, gently.

"Oh my word, yes. My Raymond looked after Kelly all her life."

"They got on well, Raymond said."

"When they were little they were inseparable. I was at work a lot and Raymond used to look after Kelly for me. A lot of people were surprised how good he was with her. They weren't even proper brother and sister. They both had different dads you see. Not that either of them are around."

She gave a forced laugh and sat down on the arm of a chair.

"I was never very lucky with men. My Raymond's dad was a long-distance lorry driver and one day he drove off to Spain and I never saw him again. My Kelly, well, I have to say, she was an accident."

She inhaled deeply from the cigarette and then slowly let the smoke escape from her mouth. Her eyes were looking past me into the far corner of the room. I thought I could just see them becoming shiny and wet again. I was about to speak when I heard the front door bell.

"Who's that?" she said, sniffing.

I looked at my watch and wondered when Raymond would get back. I walked across to the shelf of cactus plants. I couldn't resist pressing my finger against one of the thorns. It was as sharp as a pin.

Mrs Ford came back in with a young woman. She was speaking animatedly.

"Patsy, this is the Moira from Victim Support. She's been here to see me every day. I'm so grateful."

Moira smiled and held out her hand for me to

shake. I took it in a sort of awkward way. She was very thin and had closely cropped hair as though she'd gone into a barber's and had it cut. She looked familiar, and then I remembered her from the funeral. She had helped Mrs Ford down the aisle after the coffin.

"Are you one of Kelly's friends?" she said, with a sympathetic expression.

"No, Patsy's Raymond's friend," Mrs Ford said.

"Actually I ought to be going," I said, not wanting to be there when the two women started talking, "I'll catch Raymond another time."

"No, look, he's sorting some stuff out at the garage. Round the back of the flats."

"Behind the flats?" I said.

"It's the third garage along from the road end."

As I left I could see Moira walking over to the shelf of cacti.

"They're a real talking point, they are," Mrs Ford said, with a forced cheerfulness.

I felt this wave of sadness for Mrs Ford. Even with all that had happened to her she was trying to be pleasant, make small talk, make me and Moira feel at ease. I wondered if Moira knew about her drinking. With a sigh I left them both discussing the odd plant collection and let myself out.

I walked through the estate and asked a couple of kids where the garages were. They directed me and I found myself standing at the road end of a dozen or so garages that sat independently from the flats. A sign on the end said, *STORAGE SPACE TO LET, LOW RATES*.

I couldn't see Raymond Ford anywhere. I huffed with irritation. Perhaps he had gone home some other way and I had missed him. I walked up and down for a few minutes and then stopped outside the third garage from the end. The door wasn't locked but I didn't like to go in. I called out Raymond's name a couple of times. There was no answer.

Where was he?

I walked back up the line of garages and looked across the flats, the way I had come. All I could see were small knots of children playing on bikes and skateboards. I tutted. I needed to talk to him. His mum had said that Kelly was his half-sister. Whether that had any significance or not I didn't know.

I looked at my watch. Time was getting on and I still had the office accounts to do and some other phone calls to make. I'd told Joey Hooper I'd pick him up about six for a return journey to Huxley Point.

Should I wait?

I walked back down to the garage and called out Raymond's name again. Then I took the handle of the garage door and pulled it open. I'd expected it to be full of household rubbish, old bikes, suitcases, a broken fridge, boxes of tools, all that sort of stuff.

I was wrong though. There was only one thing in it.

A red hatchback car.

12

Breaking and Entering

I didn't wait for Raymond to turn up. I went straight back to work. All the way, on the tube, I kept running through the accident, trying to get a closer picture of the red car in my mind. There was nothing though. Just another car among the thousands that pass every day. It had been a red hatchback, that was all I remembered.

Raymond Ford had a red hatchback in his garage.

I remembered Carly's words: *You want to ask someone about Kelly's death, you go back and ask Raymond. He's not as soft as he looks.* Raymond had been obsessed with his sister, she had said, and he was jealous of her going out with other people. He'd even been jealous of her best friend Carly.

Then Carly was run over, almost killed by someone in a red car.

Raymond had come to me, though. He'd brought a tape from Kelly. He'd asked me to look into the murder because he thought the police had given up. Why would he have asked me to do that if he had been involved? It didn't make sense.

By the time I'd got to the office I'd been over it all a dozen times. I made myself a cup of tea and sat down to start doing the accounts, but I couldn't concentrate. Then I looked at the phone messages. I still had to decide what to do about Des Murray. I certainly wasn't ready to speak to him. I packed everything away and left a note in case my uncle came back unexpectedly.

Went home early, things to do. Patsy

Joey came out of his front door wearing jeans and a sweatshirt and looked as though he'd had a haircut. I smiled and found myself swivelling round to look at myself in the rear view mirror. I hadn't combed my hair or put on any make-up. I tutted at myself for not taking more care.

"Hi," I said, as he got in.

"All right?" he said, his hand patting his head, a little shy about his new haircut.

"I like it," I said. "You've had your 'H' put back in."

On the right side of his head, above his ear, the letter "H" had been razored in. It looked good.

"Too right. It's time I got back to my old self," he said.

He was smiling and there didn't seem to be any bad feeling about the disagreement we'd had earlier. I put the car into gear and drove off in the direction of Stratford.

The traffic was heavy and while we were inching forward, sitting in one jam after another, I told Joey about my afternoon with Mrs Ford and my discovery of the car. He was quiet, not saying much, and I wondered, yet again, whether he was still upset. Eventually, when we were almost there, he spoke.

"Did you notice a dent in the bonnet?"

"No, I didn't look," I admitted.

Of course. When the car hit Carly, it would have left a mark.

"What about the wheels? If a car stops suddenly it usually leaves a lot of tyre tread on the road. Did you notice that?"

I shook my head, dismally. I hadn't looked at the car. I'd just seen it in the garage and added up two and two.

"You need to take another look at it," he said, quietly.

"Yes," I said. "It's something else I have to talk to Raymond about."

"I don't mind coming, if you want some company."

I nodded. If Joey had been with me the first time I wouldn't have missed the obvious things.

It was near seven o'clock when we parked outside

Huxley Point. It looked busier than it had earlier in the day. There were groups of teenagers playing football on the grass area. Some young men were milling around a couple of old cars that had their bonnets up and bits of engine on the ground. Nobody looked at us as we got out of the car and walked across to the building. Once inside, a blast of music hit us and we saw two teenage girls with a portable CD player on the stairs, practising dance steps. Tucked into a corner was a pushchair with a sleeping toddler in it. They took no notice of us at all. I was beginning to see what the student with the eyebrow ring meant when she said that it was the kind of place where people minded their own business.

We took the lift up to the top floor and got out. The landing was quiet. Joey walked up to the metal grille that was across the door and lifted up the padlock.

"It doesn't look like anyone's here," he said.

"We'll wait for a bit," I said, walking out on to the stairwell and sitting on the top stair.

It was still quite light, with just the tip of a crimson red sunset over towards the city and the West End. The view was panoramic. Far down below I could see the people we'd passed, the old cars by the pavement, the football game on the grass. It looked like some tiny model city.

"There's Canary Wharf," Joey said, sitting down beside me.

I looked around to see the pointed glass roof of the skyscraper, its light blinking on and off like some giant lighthouse. My eyes jumped from it to the tall buildings of the city, the NatWest Tower and the Lloyds building. Around them, diving and circling, like persistent insects, were the red tail-lights of two helicopters.

Tracing the distance between the city and where we were sitting I noticed how the buildings got lower and older, the street patterns more complex and dense. Snaking through it all I could see the overland railway line, the sleek nose of a train moving rapidly through, passing people's houses so close that they could have reached out and touched it.

It got darker as we sat there. Looking back into the landing it was hard to pick out the front doors.

"I should have brought a torch," I said, annoyed with myself.

Joey smiled and rummaged in his rucksack. In a second he produced a black rubber torch and handed it to me.

"God. I don't seem to be able to do anything right today!" I said, clicking the button so that a tunnel of light pointed on to the landing.

Just then the grey cat appeared out of the darkness. I heard its meowing before I saw it. It came into the stairwell, brushing against my arms, keeping up its cry.

"It's probably starving," Joey said, reaching over to stroke it.

"Don't suppose you brought any cat food?" I said.

He shook his head, dolefully.

"I'll tell you one thing," I said, standing up and stretching my arms up to the ceiling, "I don't think this mystery flat-dweller is coming home."

"I suppose not," Joey said, his face filled with disappointment.

"We could always let ourselves in," I said, tentatively, not really knowing whether I had the courage to do it or not.

"Break in?"

"There's a ninety per cent chance that this flat is empty, like all the others. If so, we're not hurting anyone, all we do is close it up again. If, on the other hand, someone is living there as you said, in secret, then they're hardly likely to make a fuss if they find that someone's been there."

"What if they come along when we're in there?"

"One of us can watch, out here. Listen for the lift. We'll be in and out of there in a minute or two. Less."

"I don't know…"

"I think we should do it. See if anyone lives there. Then we'll know."

I stood up, excited by the idea.

"We haven't got any way to get in. We'd need a

wrench or something to get the padlock off," Joey said.

"I've got the very thing in the back of my car," I said, pressing the lift button, "you wait here."

"But…"

It only took a couple of minutes to go down to my car, get the monkey wrench out of the back where Billy had kindly left it for me, and go back into the building. There were a few more girls hanging around the cars but still nobody looked up or seemed interested in what I was doing. I could have had a body slung over my shoulder and no one would have batted an eyelid.

Joey was stroking the cat when I got back.

"Here," I said. "Hold the torch and I'll try and get the padlock off."

"I'm not so sure…"

The landing was almost pitch-dark and I wanted it over and done with, so that we could get away. I was getting impatient to see Raymond Ford again. I slid the wrench in behind the padlock and levered it in the opposite direction. I was amazed that after two, maybe three, goes, it came away from the wall and the metal grille hung open.

"Wow," I said.

Joey put his leg out and gave the front door a gentle kick. It swung inwards to show a pitch-black interior. It was so dark it made the landing look light by comparison. I felt a horrible unease growling around inside me. I did not feel like walking into that darkness. Joey leaned into the hallway and in a millisecond it was flooded with light.

"The electricity is on. Someone lives here, Patsy."

The cat slithered between our legs and walked confidently up the hallway of the flat. I was still worried. The bravado I had shown some minutes earlier had crumbled away.

"I'll wait out here. You go in. You know what to look for. Switch on the lights as you go in," Joey said.

"Really?" I said, handing him the torch.

"You've done stuff like this before. You told me. Anyway, I'll only be a few metres away."

He walked across to the lift and put his ear against the door.

I had no choice. I walked into the flat, not knowing what to expect. There was a hallway with four doors that opened off it. The cat had gone ahead so I followed it into the first door on the right. I turned the light on. It was a small kitchen. It was tatty but clean. On the worktop was a radio. I opened the fridge and there was a pint of milk and a packet of chocolate biscuits. Somebody was definitely living there. I held down a sense of panic. I'd done some stupid things in my time, but this was my first go at breaking and entering.

I went quickly into the second room. It was the living room. There was only an old settee and a small telly that sat on a box. What caught my eye though were the windows, which had been completely covered up with sheets of silver foil. It made sense. If someone were living there secretly they wouldn't want anyone in the outside world to see the lights on so far up the tower block. I clicked the light off and closed the door. The next door opened on to a tiny toilet and bathroom. At least, it was a toilet. There was no bath, just a space and a sink and a lot of floorboards and pipes. On the shelf above the sink I saw a couple of toothbrushes, some soap and two different hair shampoos. I let the door close and walked to the end of the hall to check on Joey.

He was standing in the beam of light that came from the hallway. He put his thumb up to indicate that all was well.

"Keep your eye on the stairs," I hissed.

The cat was still crying fiercely and it was getting on my nerves. I shooed it away with my foot and walked towards the last door. I was keen to look in and then leave, to get away back into the real world. The whole place, the flat, the tower block, was spooking me. I was about to open the last door when I saw something that made me stand completely still.

Stuck on to the door was one of those tiny porcelain name plates. The kind you buy at the seaside. They're usually white and they say things like *Jack's Room* or *Natalie's Room*.

This one said *Kelly's Room*.

"Joey," I called, my voice hesitant.

I heard his footsteps across the landing as I opened the door bit by bit. I put my hand gingerly inside and clicked the light on. I could hear Joey mumbling from behind me. The room lit up and I saw a mattress on the floor and a small chest of drawers. On the wall, above the bed there were a dozen or so photographs.

"Look at this," I said, my voice no more than a whisper.

I hadn't expected it. Not at all.

We walked carefully around the bed, looking at the pictures on the wall. A teenage girl smiling into the camera. A pretty face with light-blonde hair. A shot of her standing in front of a duck pond; another of her sitting on a swing; a couple of her in school uniform.

"Is that Kelly?" Joey said.

I nodded and looked down at the bed. On it there was a girl's nightdress, perfectly folded.

"Could she have lived here? Maybe with the boyfriend that no one knew about?"

At the side of the wall was a strip of photos, the kind you get from a booth at the station. There were four shots of Kelly and a young lad.

"Is that her and the boyfriend?" Joey said, looking over my shoulder.

"I guess so."

113

Two of the photos showed Kelly and a young lad smiling at the camera. In the others she was kissing him. The boy's hand was holding the side of her face.

"Look," I said, pointing at the boy's hand. "Look at this!"

"What?" Joey took the picture.

"He's lost one of his fingers; see, that one's been cut off." I pointed to a hand.

"It must be Liam."

"Liam Casey was going out with Kelly!"

We were both of us so absorbed that we didn't hear the lift or the footsteps down the hallway. We didn't even notice the frantic meowing of the cat. We were focused on the photos, the nightdress, the pictures on the wall of the tiny, shabby bedroom. We only heard his voice, loud and angry.

"What are you doing here?"

I turned round and saw the young man in the photo, Liam Casey, standing tall, looking hard at me and Joey, his eyes narrowed and his fists clenched at his sides.

My mouth fell open but no words came out.

13

Liam Casey

Liam Casey snatched the photos from my hand, then he shoved Joey out of the way.

"Wait," I said, "I can explain!"

Joey stood up to his full height though and pushed Liam hard on the chest. Liam almost stumbled, but held his footing, grabbed Joey's sweatshirt and pushed him hard up against the wall. Then he drew his fist back and punched him. It happened in a flash. All the time I was saying, "Stop it now, come on, stop it please." All I could hear was grunting and I could see Joey using his forearms to lever Liam away. In a second Joey was free and I saw his fist spring out at Liam. It caught him on the side of the face and he fell back on to the bed.

"Oh no," I said, my throat croaking, "I can explain…"

As Liam pushed himself up and back towards Joey, I remembered watching the video where Dan Mackenzie and Vincent Black had been fighting. I had this terrible sense of dejà vu. It could happen again, bad injuries coming from a fight, just a couple of lads throwing some punches. I pushed myself between the two of them. Joey was at my back. Liam was in front of me, his chin looking red, his eyes full of fury.

"For God's sake stop it the two of you, STOP IT!" I screamed.

Liam looked at me in an astonished way. I turned round and pushed Joey away. He was trembling and I could see some blood on his cheekbone.

"I can explain," I said, turning back to Liam. "When you hear what I've got to say you'll know we weren't just nosing around."

"Careful Patsy, this guy's got an iron punch."

"Patsy?" Liam said, looking puzzled. "Are you the Patsy that Kelly wrote to? The one she read about in the paper?"

"That's me," I said, still trembling.

"Why didn't you say?"

"I tried to!"

Liam Casey slumped back against the wall, his face all closed up. He looked at me and then Joey. Then he rubbed his chin where Joey had hit him. I kept talking, my words falling over each other.

"We found this place by accident. We were asking

around to see if anyone had remembered anything about the day Kelly was killed. Joey saw the different padlock and we noticed the cat. We didn't know it was you who lived here."

Liam Casey looked suspiciously at Joey.

"What's he got to do with it?"

"This is my friend, Joey Hooper," I said.

I looked round at Joey and saw, with dismay, that blood was trickling down his cheek. I patted my pockets to find a tissue but I didn't have one. Liam saw me and went to a drawer. He pulled out a wad of tissues and threw them on the bed.

"Thanks a lot," Joey said, sarcastically.

I looked at them both in agitation. If anything positive was going to come out of the situation I had to get them both to be civil towards each other.

"Any chance of a cup of tea?" I said, in a mildly hysterical voice.

Liam, who was still looking aggravated, gave a half-nod and walked out of the room and towards the kitchen. I turned to Joey.

"He was Kelly's boyfriend! This is a big development. Try and be nice to him!" I hissed the words, like a command.

Joey dabbed at the blood on his face.

"He's the one with the sledgehammer fist, not me."

I squatted down and tidied the bed, folding Kelly's nightdress up. When I stood up I looked closely at

117

Joey's cheek. It was a nasty cut but it looked like the blood was drying up.

"Are you all right?" I said, gently, my hand on his shoulder.

"I'll live," he said.

In the kitchen Liam had fed the cat. It was crouched over its bowl eating ravenously. Every now and then it stopped, looked up, and eyed us all suspiciously.

"What's it called?" I said.

"Nothing. It's a stray. I should really stop feeding it, then it would go away," Liam said, his voice still sulky.

He had two mugs and a cup out on the worktop. In each of them was a tea bag. He kept himself busy putting the cat food in the fridge, getting the milk out, washing a spoon, waiting for the kettle to boil. He gave Joey a sideways look but said nothing. All the time I looked at him. He was smaller than I'd imagined and quite thin, his jeans and T-shirt looking loose. His mousy hair was hanging in his eyes as he bent over the worktop. Every now and again he used his fingers like a comb to move it back only to find it falling forward again. I couldn't help but focus on the missing fourth finger. While he was pouring the boiling water on to the tea bags I decided to start talking.

"Why do you live *here*?"

"What's it to you? What's any of this got to do with you?" he said, angry again.

I didn't speak. I began to think we weren't going to get anything out of him. I bent over and ran the backs of my fingers against the cat. *Give him time*, I said to myself. After a few minutes' uncomfortable silence he spoke.

"I've been in this building a couple of months. I don't get on with my mum's new husband. I know these flats because my cousins used to live here. I needed a place, it wasn't that hard to get in, get the electricity and water back on. I know a few people and they helped me out."

I nodded my head.

"Doesn't anyone know you're here?" Joey said.

"I'm not always here. Sometimes I stay with mates. Even so, living all the way up here it's easy to keep out of people's way. At least I thought so up to now. Exactly what are you and him doing here?"

"I got Kelly's letter and tried to ring her but there was no answer." I explained. "When I found out she was dead I passed it on to the police. I've never been officially involved in this case, but a couple of days ago Raymond Ford came to see me with a cassette tape that Kelly had made a while ago, in which she says she was scared of Vincent Black. He wanted me to find out more."

"You're on the wrong track. Vince didn't have anything to do with it. I'm not surprised that Raymond is going round saying he did. Raymond is a seriously weird guy."

"Why do you say that?"

"Because Kelly was desperate to get away from him."

I'd heard this from Carly Dickens just before she'd been run over by a red hatchback.

"Why?" Joey said.

"He had a strange attitude towards her. You wouldn't think she was his sister."

He handed me a mug of tea and Joey the small cup. Then he leaned back on the side. I'd thought he was going to open up, to start talking, but he lapsed into silence. Sometimes, getting people to share their story with you was hard work.

"I was in prison with Vince Black," Joey said, breaking the silence. "He was always talking about you. He said you were a hard man and you'd do anything for him."

Liam looked up from his tea and pushed his hair back with his fingers. A smile spread across his face.

"Vince lived in a dreamworld. He thought he was king of the streets. That's why he ended up inside. I'm no hard man. I've never deliberately picked a fight with anyone…"

"It felt like a fight to me," Joey said, touching his swollen cheekbone.

"You were in my flat. In me and Kelly's bedroom. I didn't know…"

"Vince said that you cut your finger off because he told you to," Joey went on.

"Vince is all talk. Haven't you worked that out yet? That wasn't how it happened. We were cleaning his dad's car. We were both about ten. He slammed the door on my hand. As simple as that. An accident."

"Oh," I said.

"I don't know how the story started. I don't know if Vince told it or someone else exaggerated it. All I know is that when Vince was bragging he liked to tell it his way. Sometimes I contradicted him. Not always."

"What about you and Kelly?" I said.

Once he'd started talking I wanted to keep him going. He looked hard at me and I thought that he was going to tell me to mind my own business. Eventually he put his mug of tea down and spoke.

"I went to see Vince a couple of months after he got sent down. He was sure that Kelly was playing around with someone. He asked me to find out. Actually he told me to find the guy and sort him out. Like I said, Vince thought he was the top man and I was a kind of bodyguard. I could have told him to grow up, but he was depressed enough already. I thought to myself, it'll all blow over in a few weeks and they'll be back together again."

Joey and me kept quiet. Myself, I could see where the story was going, but I wanted to hear Liam tell it.

"So I saw Kelly. We talked. I told her what Vince

thought, what he said. She was adamant that there was no one. I believed her. I told Vince but he wouldn't have it."

He stopped for a minute and drank his tea. The cat had finished its meal and was sitting at Liam's feet, licking its paws.

"We went out together one night. We got on well. She told me about how trapped she felt with Vince. Especially since the kid's death. She said her feelings for him had changed, that she was afraid of him and was dreading the time when he came out of prison."

He shrugged his shoulders.

"That was how it started. We just got on well."

"Weren't you worried about Vince?"

"What could he do? If it hadn't been me it would have been someone else. Kelly was never going to go back to him. I didn't worry about it. I decided to face him with it when he came out of prison. There was no point in him knowing before then. Kelly was scared though. She worried about it all the time."

"Because he'd threatened her?"

"I tried to calm her down. She thought he had spies on her. She said she was being followed. Half the time I thought she imagined it. She'd make these elaborate arrangements for us to meet, a long way from here. Then she'd arrive and tell me that there was a red car following her. I never saw it. Not once. Then she said she used to get these funny phone calls. She was a bundle of nerves. That's why she wrote to you."

"Is that why she moved in here?"

"Partly. That and she wanted to get away from Raymond."

"Why?"

"She said he used to watch her. She even thought *he* was following her at one time. I thought to myself, it's all in her mind, she's getting paranoid. But then she told me that she went into his room one day and found some of her clothes crumpled up under his pillow. As if he'd been sleeping with them."

"Why didn't she tell her mum?"

"He was her brother. She just couldn't." He shook his head. "It got really difficult. It made sense for her to get out of the way for a while. I thought she would calm down a bit being here."

"Were you here when it happened?" Joey said.

"I'd been doing a bit of casual work, in a garden centre off the A13. I left there about one and I was supposed to come straight back to the flat, but the truth was Kelly and I had had a row. I was fed up with her moaning and jumping out of her skin every time I came through the door. She kept talking about coming clean, telling Vince about us, getting it all out into the open. I was fed up with it. After work I went for a walk along the river. I got back to the flats about three. There was still a crowd and lots of talk about what had happened. Some girl's jumped off the top, someone said. I couldn't believe it. I was nearly sick. I had to sit down."

"Why didn't you go to the police?" I said.

"I was in shock. I walked around till about ten o'clock. I went back to my mum's house. I just wasn't thinking straight. I thought to myself, they'll think it's me. They'll find out what Vince asked me to do and they'll believe it. I had no alibi."

I could see that it might look bad for him.

"I thought, I'll wait until they arrest someone. Then I'll go and see them. But they never did and the longer I left it the more guilty I looked. Then I read this report in the paper. It said the police were considering suicide."

He stopped speaking and put his hand over his mouth. I thought for a minute he was going to cry. He seemed to steel himself though, and carried on.

"And I thought, it's my fault. I brought her here. I ignored the fact that she was scared. I had a row with her that morning and told her to pull herself together. If she committed suicide then I was the one to blame."

He looked waxy and I noticed then, under the bare light bulb, that he had dark circles under his eyes...

"That's not true," I said, "I don't think it was suicide at all..."

I stopped speaking because I was about to

mention the Carly Dickens hit-and-run. I wasn't sure though that he knew about it and I didn't want to upset him any more. Joey seemed to have read my mind.

"Look at it logically, Liam. Kelly was being stalked. Then she was dead. You add those two things up and you don't get suicide."

Liam looked at him and nodded his head slowly.

"That's why it's so important to find out if anyone saw anything here, on that day. That's why we ended up breaking into your flat. We don't believe it's suicide or we wouldn't be here!"

I said it with feeling. I wanted to convince him that we were on his side.

He reached over and picked up the cups. The interview was over.

"We should go anyway," I said.

He mumbled something without turning around.

"Here," I said, tearing a scrap of paper out of my notebook. "This is my mobile phone number. If you want to contact me, or you think of anything that might be important, you could ring me."

I held it out to him but he didn't take it. I let it drop on to the worktop.

"Come on, Patsy, let's go," Joey said, opening the door.

"And you're absolutely sure no one knew about this place? I mean, what about your family or your old friends?" I tried.

One last question. One little piece of information like a tiny key that might unlock the case.

He didn't answer, just stood with his back to us. His shoulders were hunched and I wondered if he was actually crying. I left him there and walked out along the hall to the landing.

"He's still in shock," Joey said, rubbing at the cut on his cheek.

I nodded as we walked down the stairs, the lights of East London twinkling below us.

14

Working Close

It was nine-thirty as we drove away from Huxley Point. As I was sitting waiting to turn a corner I looked back over my shoulder to the tower block. The bottom half of it was dotted with lights. There was nothing above that.

"Do you think I should have told him about Carly Dickens?"

"Hard to say," Joey said.

I felt disgruntled.

"There's lots of things I still need to know about the flats. I should have asked him while I had the chance. I should have made a list."

"How could you? You didn't know you were going to see him."

"What about the door to the roof? Was it always

open? Or easy to open?"

"Perhaps it wasn't a concern, seeing that no one lived up that high."

"And what about the flat? After Kelly died. It wasn't discovered by the police. So it must have been locked up? Who locked it up? I should have asked Liam!"

"Give him a bit of time to calm down. You can see him again."

"I hope he doesn't wait too long. I can't hold off going to see Des Murray for ever."

"Why don't we go and see Raymond Ford? Ask him about that red car."

Joey was right. Even though I was tired, I was feeling exhilarated. There were little bits of the case that were unravelling; tiny threads hanging temptingly. Mrs Ford would have told Raymond that I'd visited. She would have also told him that I'd gone looking for him round at the garage. It was as well to see him quickly before he had time to realize that anything was wrong.

"Are you sure you don't mind?" I said, suddenly aware that I was using up a lot of Joey's time.

"It's fine. I'm enjoying it. Sort of."

He put his hand on the back of my neck and rubbed it for a millisecond. It gave me a warm shivery feeling. I didn't know what to say or how to respond. I reached across and clicked the radio on. The car filled with music and he sat back and closed his eyes. I kept my eyes on the road and we drove to Stratford without speaking.

Raymond Ford opened the front door. He didn't smile when he saw me. His shoulders were rounded and he was peering out into the street behind us. Just as his mother had done earlier on.

"How come you came to see my mum?" he demanded, keeping us standing on the front door. "Who's he?" he added, pointing his thumb at Joey.

"I didn't come to see your mum, I came to see you. You rang me, remember? And this is my friend, Joey Hooper. Joey, this is Raymond Ford."

I said it sarcastically. For someone who came to my office and asked me to get involved in the case he was certainly not looking very pleased to see me.

"You didn't have to come here. I don't want my mum any more upset than she already is."

He was holding tightly on to the front door as though he was afraid we might force our way in.

"I didn't upset her, Raymond. I just waited for you. When you didn't come I went round to the garages, but you weren't there either so I went back to the office."

He looked at me and then Joey. He was thinking about it.

"Can't we talk?" I said in a friendly voice.

"No," he said, "that's why I rang you today. I don't need you. I saw a police officer called Murray this afternoon. He's dealing with it."

Des Murray was still looking into the case. That was something.

"Can't you at least invite us in for a cup of tea?"

"No. I was wrong to come to you. I should have gone straight to the police. Now I'm dealing with them."

And the front door shut.

I looked at Joey with surprise. I had expected Raymond Ford to be guarded, difficult even, but I hadn't expected him to refuse to speak to us.

"Let's go," Joey said, and pulled my arm back in the direction of the car.

"But what about the garages?" I hissed.

"We'll drive round the block. He'll think we've left. Then we can cut back and look at the garage."

It was a sensible suggestion. I walked to the car and got in. I looked back up at the Fords' house and thought, for a second, that I had seen someone looking out of the upstairs front window.

"He's got something to hide," Joey said as we moved off.

"Then why come to me and ask me to get involved?"

"A double bluff?"

"What do you mean?"

"Let's say that Raymond Ford had this obsession for his sister. He liked to look after her; he liked to be with her; he liked to sleep with her clothes under his pillow. Then she leaves home without telling him. Somehow he finds out where she is. He follows her and decides that if he can't have her all to himself then no one will. He takes her up to the roof and pushes her off."

"How did he know where she was? No one knew…"

"I'm just playing around with ideas, Patsy."

I pulled into a parking spot about a hundred metres away from the garages.

"OK, so he's killed her and he wants to avoid getting caught for it. He waits to see if the police have anyone. When they don't he realizes that he's still in danger of being a suspect. So he goes to you and demands that the case is opened up. He insists that the police find the killer and get the ball rolling again. So this Des Murray is going to knock Raymond Ford right off his list of suspects, precisely because he has fought to keep the case open."

I didn't say anything for a minute, because it was an intriguing idea.

"What about Carly Dickens? Why run her over?"

"She knew something? He blamed her for the way his sister had turned out? He'd killed once and decided to do it again?"

I sat for a minute. Could Carly have known something about Kelly's death? That would be the only thing that would explain Raymond trying to get rid of her. I leaned over to the back seat and picked up the monkey wrench that I'd used earlier. Joey gave me a quizzical look.

"We might have to break in again," I said.

"Right. Two counts of Breaking and Entering in one night. And I said I was going straight!" he said, taking the wrench from me.

I watched him get out of the car and felt this rush of admiration for him. He'd been a real pal, dropping everything to help me out. Then I felt a niggle of guilt. If it hadn't been for the case I wouldn't have called him as soon as I did. Was that all he was? Someone to share the case with? Someone to take Billy's place?

I remembered his hand on the back of my neck and the feel of his fingers on my skin, and I was momentarily confused. Joey Hooper was a friend, wasn't he? A knock on the window shook me out of my thoughts and I got out of the car and followed him.

The garages were deserted, lit up only by the distant street lights. Joey got his torch out and we walked along until we came to the right door. We stood for a minute looking around to make sure that no one was near. In the adjacent flats I could hear distant sounds of TVs and hi-fis. From somewhere over to my right I could hear the sound of a motor-bike revving up, a thin buzzing sound like a giant insect that grated on my nerves.

I took the monkey wrench out of my jacket and put it behind the padlock. In my head I was hoping, willing, the car in the garage to be the one that knocked Carly down. How neat it would all be. A jealous brother who loved his sister too much. The red hatchback showing the signs of a hit-and-run. It would be perfect.

The padlock was harder to get off than the one in Huxley Point. I took great breaths of air and forced the wrench as hard as I could. In the end I stood back and let Joey have a go. I looked around while he concentrated and put all his weight on the wrench. It suddenly came loose and before either of us could catch it, it clattered on to the concrete making a noise that seemed to be as loud as a bell ringing.

We both stood rigidly still, Joey's eyes catching mine, one of his fingers over his lips. When no one came running from the flats or from the street we relaxed and went back to the garage door. I had one last look around before signalling to Joey to pull the wooden door open.

Inside it was pitch-dark and Joey clicked his torch on. It threw a powerful beam of light into the garage.

There was nothing there. No car, nothing.

"Are you sure this is the right one?" Joey whispered.

I was sure. I took a few steps back and looked at the door. As if we could be wrong. It was the third garage from the end. The same one that I had looked in earlier, when I had seen a red hatchback car.

"Did you look in the right one this afternoon?" he said, backing out of the empty garage.

"Yes," I hissed. "Yes, I'm sure."

But suddenly I wasn't sure. I tried to trace back my steps, walking up and down the garages, looking for Raymond, opening the door of the garage. Yes, it was the third one from the road. Wasn't it?

I didn't have time to think any more. A siren sounded in the near distance, piercing through me. I looked round, at the dark street and at the flats above. There wasn't a soul around.

"Someone's called the police!" Joey hissed as the siren seemed to move in our direction.

"Oh no." The words dropped out of my mouth like great weights.

"Quick, we'll have to run," Joey said, "if they catch me I'm straight back in the nick."

"OK," I said, grabbing the monkey wrench and pushing it under my jacket.

The sound of the siren was just metres away and the headlights of the police car swung across the garages just as we ran into the dark shadows. We heard car doors slamming and the abrupt stop of the siren. The words, "Stop, we're police!" rang in my ears and I grabbed Joey's hand as we fled through the alleyways between the flats.

"Quick, in here," Joey said as we came to a garden.

We stood behind a tree close together, watching to see if the police were still following us. A moment later I heard their feet coming along the alleyway, one of them shouting, "Stop, police officers!"

Then they ran past us, only glancing sideways at the garden, not noticing us hardly breathing, sandwiched together behind the tree. Their footsteps receded into the distance and I literally fell against Joey with relief, the monkey wrench dropping out from underneath my coat on to the grass. We had got away with it. That's what I thought. I had even taken a couple of steps away from the tree when I heard them again.

"They're coming back," Joey whispered, looking frantically around the garden for some way of escape.

I looked at him with alarm. His earlier words had only just registered. If he got picked up by the police he would go straight back to prison. There was no question about it.

The voices got louder and I stood with my back to the tree waiting for them to come and find us. Joey was a couple of metres away looking distraught. It was only a matter of a few seconds more and we would be caught. He walked towards me and I felt about as bad as I could possibly feel. I was about to open my mouth to say sorry to him when he put his arms around me and his head into my neck. Then he whispered, "Kiss me and make it look good."

I was shocked and stood with my mouth open for a second as the police officers appeared in the alleyway.

Then I pulled him towards me, closed my eyes and kissed him as hard as I could. I felt him move closer and I did the same, my hands running up and down his back. We were only play-acting, I said to myself. I stopped for a second then turned my head to the side and kissed him again.

In the background I could hear the voices of the police officers, "What have we got here, a couple of lovebirds?"

I didn't stop. I knew it was important to be convincing and I pushed my hand into Joey's short thick hair and found my fingers outlining the "H" he had had razored into the side.

"Oi, you two, did you see anyone running past here, about three or four minutes ago?"

Joey stopped kissing and stood looking at me, his eyes crinkling up at the corners. I grinned at him, my mouth still half-open.

"Sorry officer, what did you say?" Joey said, turning to look at them.

They were both male and one of them was looking me up and down while the other spoke to Joey. I looked away and saw that the monkey wrench was lying on the grass in full view. My heart seemed to take a leap up into my throat.

"A couple of kids broke into the garages down the

way. We followed them along here. Did you see anyone?"

"Sorry officer. We've been a bit busy."

The officer gave a broad smile and then shrugged his shoulders. The other one had turned away and was talking into a radio. Neither of them were looking at the grass where the wrench was lying.

"Probably well away by now."

He pushed his partner on the shoulder and they started to walk back in the direction they'd come from.

"We'd better hang on a bit," Joey said, "give them time to get away."

I nodded, leaning back against the tree again, a whole swirl of emotions racing round inside my chest. We had done it. We had fooled them. Joey bent down and picked up the monkey wrench. Then he stood in front of me, where he'd been before. I looked at him and felt a flood of desire.

"Maybe we'd better make it look good," I whispered, taking his arms and pulling him back towards me.

"If you say so, Patsy," he said, and kissed me on the mouth.

When we got back to the car the street was quiet. It was almost midnight and a lot of the lights were off. I looked over at the garages and remembered with dismay that the red car hadn't been there.

"No red car," I whispered.

Joey Hooper had his arm round me.

"He's moved it," he said. "Tomorrow I'll watch him. See if he doesn't go and pick it up from somewhere."

I nodded my head gratefully. It would give me a chance to get on with other things.

"Come on," I said, "it's time to go home."

15

The Letter

The next morning, after a restless night's sleep, I forced myself to sit down and eat a piece of toast. I chewed each bite calmly while inside my head a film was running. It was a jumbled replay of the events of the night before: the kiss, the car, Huxley Point, Liam Casey, Canary Wharf, the chase, the monkey wrench, Raymond Ford, the red car, the police siren, the missing red car, the chase, the kiss.

The Kisschase.

There it was, firmly in my head, like a game that children play. I closed my eyes and remembered the moment when Joey had whispered in my ear *kiss me and make it look good*. It had started as a ploy, a way of throwing the police officers off the scent. But it had ended differently with me clinging on to Joey, feeling his mouth on my skin, his fingers teasing through my hair.

"Patsy!"

I opened my eyes to see my mum standing by the kitchen table. On my plate was a half-eaten piece of toast. There was pop music coming from the radio behind me. It took me a second to register where I was, what time of the day it was, what my mum was saying. She had something blue in her hand.

"Patsy, wake up. You're in a daydream. Here's your letter from Billy. You've waited for it long enough."

My throat seemed to shrivel as I took the envelope with its dark blue and red piping. On the front of it was Billy's neat handwriting. *Ms Patsy Kelly*, it said and after it he'd drawn three Xs. Three kisses for me. I looked hard at the envelope and tried to swallow a few times. Then my vision became blurred and I knew I was going to cry.

"Honestly!" my mum said.

I left the toast and went up to my own room. I sat on the bed and pulled the duvet up around me. Then I opened the letter, my fingers trembling.

Dear Patsy, it started, *I've missed you so much. In the first couple of days I was on the brink of buying a ticket and flying back home again. The only thing that stopped me was the thought that I would let everyone down, even you. What would you have thought if I'd crept back home having achieved nothing?*

I kept reading even though there was a great heaviness pressing down on my shoulders.

I arrived in Angola at ten o'clock in the morning their time...

The letter ran for four pages. I read it over twice. After arrival Billy spent four days in transit, staying overnight in hostels while his placement was finalized. He was with some other young people, a couple and some lads from Yorkshire. They'd been put on a coach, and then a minibus and finally, when they left the towns behind, a Range Rover.

Every couple of paragraphs Billy seemed to remember that I was still living in London, getting on with my day to day life.

How are your mum and Gerry? Is the wedding going ahead? How's uncle Tony? Has he managed to set up his web page? Any new cases? Make sure you go out a bit, don't sit indoors all the time pining for me!

I looked at the exclamation mark. He was joking, being ironic. I let the letter drop out of my hand.

If only it had come yesterday. Then I would have read it with glee, taking delight in all the minute details of his experience. I would have bristled with pleasure at the kisses and endearments and the line at the end that said, *I love you lots, don't forget me, Billy.*

Instead I was racked with guilt, my emotions retreating into a dark corner, my fists clenched with shame.

I sat like that for a long time unable to pull myself together. I had things to do, I knew that. I had planned to go to the London Hospital and find out how Carly Dickens was. I had to go into the office. At some point I simply had to go and see Des Murray and fill him in on the stuff that I'd found out.

Somewhere in that itinerary I had to see Joey Hooper. He was going to watch Raymond Ford and see if he went to collect the red car. He would ring me on his mobile, he'd said, if anything developed. Since Billy's letter I almost dreaded speaking to him again.

I stood up and walked to the window. I had to pull myself together, get things into perspective. The stuff between Joey and me, it hadn't meant anything. We had both been caught in a whirlpool of emotions; fear of being caught, utter relief, total exhilaration. We'd just fallen headlong into each other's arms.

That was what had happened and I would be absolutely straight with him about it. He knew I had a boyfriend. He wouldn't be surprised. I just hoped that it wouldn't affect our friendship.

I felt better immediately. I picked up Billy's letter and tucked it behind my clock radio. I opened my wardrobe door and took out a long skirt and blouse that were quite smart. Then I sorted out a shoulder bag and a pair of loafers, some earrings and my make-up bag.

It didn't hurt to make an effort.

* * *

My uncle was at his desk when I got to the office. He didn't look best pleased to see me.

"You've decided to put in an appearance then?" He shoved a piece of paper at me. On it was written *RING DES MURRAY!!!!*

"I'm sorry I've not been around a lot. I've been working on the Kelly Ford case."

There, I'd said it. I folded the piece of paper in half and then half again. As if by doing it I could hide Des Murray away.

Tony sat back in his chair and looked at me with mild exasperation. Then he picked up a nail file and played around with the edge of his thumb.

"Is that wise?" he said.

"She wrote to me. It was my case. I should have done something about it then. I didn't, so I'm doing something about it now."

Holding the nail file out he pointed to a chair.

"Tell me what you've got so far."

I sat down slowly. I didn't want to involve him but I started talking anyway. I told him about Raymond Ford and his obsession with his sister. I described talking to Carly Dickens and her being run over by a red car. I told him what I'd seen in Raymond Ford's garage and watched his eyebrows move with interest. I went on to our visit to Huxley Point, finding Liam Casey there. Finally I told him that the car had disappeared.

It was a selective version of events. I'd left out a lot of stuff, especially anything to do with Breaking and Entering. He pursed his lips and looked as though he was thinking hard. I was half waiting for a lecture on leaving it to the professionals or not working on cases where we weren't getting paid. He looked me up and down. My hair was done, I had make-up on and my clothes were smart. I even had a shoulder bag instead of a rucksack. He obviously came to a decision because he made a great show of tapping keys and moving his mouse.

"Is there anything you want me to do?" he said.

"You could keep Des Murray off my back," I said, tentatively.

"You're withholding information," he said, the retired policeman inside him waking up.

"There's nothing firm," I hedged. "If I go to Des Murray with any of this he'll laugh me out of the station. You know he hates me."

"You'll have to see him sometime."

"By tomorrow I should have something more concrete."

"Tomorrow. I'll keep Murray off your back until tomorrow afternoon. Five o'clock. We'll go to the station together."

"OK," I said, warily, waiting for the catch.

All I heard was the tapping of the keys and my uncle humming something lightly under his breath. It was a strange moment. My uncle Tony, Private

Investigator, was letting me go, was trusting me to do something by myself, even helping me to thwart the authorities.

It was a mystery, but I didn't have time to worry about it.

I left my car at Stratford and got the tube to the London Hospital. Outside the underground station were about a dozen market stalls, some selling exotic fruits and vegetables, spices and flowers and plants; others selling clothes and records and household items. There was music coming from all directions, different sounds mingling into a cacophony of rhythms. I decided to buy a bunch of flowers from a stall.

I walked into the hospital not knowing whether Carly was conscious or not, or whether I'd even be able to see her. At the reception desk a stern-looking, grey-haired woman tapped into a computer and told me that she had been admitted to St John's ward on the fifth floor.

I waited for the lift behind several medical people and a man in a wheelchair. It had only been a couple of days since I had last stood there, on my way to see Heather after her miscarriage. I wondered how she was and couldn't help remembering her un-controlled sobs as she lay on her hospital bed. She hadn't wanted the pregnancy, not at first. It wouldn't have fitted with her lifestyle: Detective

Inspector Heather Warren, a senior woman in the police force; a single mother.

The lift finally came and I squeezed in.

What if Heather hadn't had the miscarriage? I smiled to myself for a minute. I imagined her driving in a squad car with a tiny baby in a seat beside her. I pictured her sitting in the CID room, a baby at her breast, discussing the details of some grisly crime. I was being silly, I knew.

On the other hand I had this feeling that Heather would have managed. She would have resumed her job, insisting on things like childcare provision and sensible working hours. She'd probably have hosted workshops on *The Single Mother in the Modern Police Force*.

I resolved to go and see her as soon as she was well enough.

When I got to the ward I stood for a moment looking around. A couple of nurses were making a bed in a side room. One of them, a small, thin woman with deep lines in her forehead, tutted to herself and pointed to a notice that said *Visiting hours 12 until 8*. It was 10.40.

"I'm just delivering the flowers," I said cheerfully, holding up my bunch for view.

She mumbled to herself crossly and turned away, punching a few pillows.

I found my way round several small side wards, and finally spotted Carly Dickens. She was lying down with her shoulder in plaster, and her arm held in mid-air by wires attached to weights.

I tiptoed quietly along, not wanting to disturb any of the other patients. When I was a few steps away I could see that her face was a mix of purples and blues, and the white of one of her eyes was shot through with blood. She turned her head for a moment and I saw then that some her hair had been shaved, and there was a wound on her head that had been stitched. She looked awful.

"Carly," I whispered, laying the flowers on a trolley at the end of her bed.

Her eyes opened slowly and she looked around for a moment before focusing on me. Then her forehead creased up and she closed and opened her eyes again. She didn't know who I was.

"Carly, do you remember me? I'm Patsy. I gave you a lift from work the night of the accident. You were talking to me about Kelly Ford."

"I remember you," she said, dully, her eyes settling on me. "What do you want?"

I sat down, not encouraged by her tone.

"How are you?" I said.

She pulled herself up on the pillow slightly, her spare hand holding on to the other shoulder. It was then I noticed that her front teeth had been smashed and that there was dried blood on the pillow where she'd lain.

"Hey, I've never been better," she said getting

herself into a more comfortable position.

"What do the doctors say?"

"Not much. A dislocated shoulder, two broken ribs, concussion, eight stitches in a head wound, cuts and bruises. I'll be up and playing tennis in a few days."

"Do you remember anything about it?"

"I'm walking along, on my way home. Next thing I know there's a nurse taking my temperature and I've got a terrible headache."

The woman in the next bed was flicking through a magazine and watching a small portable TV set at the same time. From time to time I saw her eyes swivelling in our direction. Behind me, I could hear the murmur of the nurses moving towards us. Any minute they would notice me and I'd have to go. I didn't have time for small talk.

"Do you remember us talking about Raymond Ford?"

Carly's lips twitched and she reached out to her bedside table and pulled a tissue out of a box.

"I'm laid up here and all you can think about is Raymond Ford!"

"It's important," I said. "Don't you think it's funny? Kelly is killed, and then you are knocked down in what looks like a deliberate hit-and-run."

"The police didn't say anything about it being deliberate," Carly said.

"You said, that night in the car, that Raymond

didn't like you being Kelly's friend. What did you mean?"

Carly Dickens gave a great sigh.

"You're wasting your time," she said. "What are you saying? Raymond ran me over?"

I didn't speak. I couldn't commit myself.

"You think Raymond killed his sister and then ran me over?"

I wasn't getting anywhere. Every time I asked a question she answered with another. On the spur of the moment I decided to try a new direction. It would all come out in the next couple of days anyway.

"Did you know that Kelly had been seeing Liam Casey? That she was with him the week before she died?"

Carly lay very still for a few moments, her face giving nothing away. Then she put the back of her hand up to her eyes. I couldn't tell for sure but I thought she was crying. I felt the tiniest sting of remorse.

"I'm sorry, it must be upsetting for you."

"Come on," she said, after a couple of sniffs into the tissue. "It's not like Kelly was the most loyal person in the world. Look at how she dropped Vince as soon as he went inside."

"You and Liam had finished some time before," I said.

"You've seen Liam?" she said. "Does he know

about me? That I'm in hospital?"

She looked straight at me for the first time since I'd got there. Her sarcasm had gone and in its place was a real need, a look of desperation.

"I never told him," I said, shrugging.

She closed her eyes again.

"Why don't you clear off. I'm tired."

"Carly, somebody tried to kill you. Don't you care?"

I whispered the words with urgency in my voice. From behind me I heard the rattle of a trolley and I turned to see the nurses coming towards Carly's bed. The small thin one gave an exaggerated look at her watch. I had no choice. I would have to go. I patted the flowers that I'd brought and then I said my goodbyes. I don't even think that Carly opened her eyes as I walked away.

Going down in the lift I felt disappointed. I'd learned nothing more about Raymond. All I knew was what Liam had told me the night before. Everything now rested on finding the red car.

Oddly, in spite of myself, I felt some sympathy for the brash, sarcastic redhead who was lying injured in the bed upstairs. I pictured her face as I'd told her about Liam and Kelly. There had been a look of real desolation.

Something occurred to me then. I'd asked Carly if she'd known about Kelly and Liam. She'd not spoken at first but then she'd said something about

Kelly not being very loyal. She hadn't actually answered my question. She'd been upset, moved to tears but she hadn't been shocked. She hadn't said, *You're kidding! You're not serious! Not Liam and Kelly, no, I don't believe it!*

Carly Dickens had known that Kelly was seeing Liam.

How had she found out? Had Kelly confided in her best friend? Had she thought that it had been over between Carly and Liam so long that it wouldn't matter? Or had Carly seen them together somewhere? Walking along the street, holding hands, kissing? I didn't know the answer.

With these thoughts in my mind I made my way back to the tube station.

16

Complaints

The office was in an uproar when I got back. My uncle Tony was standing near my desk in front of two women, one of whom I recognized immediately as Mrs Ford.

"What's going on?" I said.

"This is the woman I want to complain about," Mrs Ford said, pointing dramatically at me. She was wobbling slightly and her cheeks were flushed.

The other woman, who I then recognized as the Victim Support person, put her arm around Mrs Ford and made shushing sounds. My uncle was looking pained.

"Mrs Ford, I really do wish you would calm yourself. I'm sure that my operative, Miss Kelly, had no intention of upsetting your son."

"She came to my house under false pretences!" she said, leaning back against a chair.

She'd been drinking, I was sure. The woman from Victim Support, who I remembered was called Moira, pulled a chair out and made Mrs Ford sit down. She had her hand on the older woman's shoulder, long thin fingers patting her as though she was a troubled child.

"I've just lost my daughter," she said, "and now my son is harassed by this woman."

"Now Maureen, you don't know if that's absolutely true," Moira said.

"Why don't I make a nice cup of tea?" my uncle said.

"She interrogated me, you know. While my Raymond was out. 'Was Raymond close to his sister?' she said, and I answered freely. She took me for a fool!"

"Mrs Ford, I'm sorry, I really was looking for Raymond. I never meant to offend you."

Mrs Ford's eyes became glassy and her shoulders began to shake.

"I've just lost my daughter…" she said in a thin whine. Then she broke into great sobs.

Moira crouched down and took Mrs Ford's hands in hers and spoke to her in a low, calm voice. My uncle Tony started to tidy up a tray of paper clips. I stood looking lost.

"I'll make that tea," I said, as though everything was normal.

A while later we all sat in Tony's office drinking from china cups and saucers. In the middle was a plate of pink wafer biscuits that no one had touched. My uncle had been saying how upset we were when we heard about Kelly's death. Moira had been comforting Mrs Ford all the while. She was doing a really good job, I thought. I remembered then that Victim Support was a voluntary organization; just like the one Billy had gone to work for. I felt a pang of guilt remembering his letter and the business with Joey. It seemed, at the moment, as though I wasn't able to please anybody.

"Mrs Ford, Raymond rang me. I only came to your house because I thought he wanted to see me."

Her face calmer, Mrs Ford looked over the top of her cup without speaking.

"He asked me to help!" I said, looking beseechingly at Moira.

"He did tell you that," Moira said to Mrs Ford.

"I know," she sniffed, "it's just that I thought you were his friend. Otherwise I wouldn't have discussed his — our — life with you. Especially personal things about him and Kelly. No, not at all."

"I'm sorry if I upset you. It's just that a couple of the people I've spoken to have suggested that Raymond had ... well ... that he was ... a bit too close with his sister. I just wanted to find out if it was an exaggeration."

"Who said that?" she said, looking suddenly nasty.

"I would have asked him if he had been there. I wasn't doing anything behind his back…"

I said it nervously. I didn't want to upset her any more. I looked at my uncle, expecting him to be glaring at me, but he was looking intently at Mrs Ford.

"I know what this is!" she said, her cup clattering into the saucer. "I know where this comes from. Carly Dickens. She's told you this, hasn't she? She's poisonous, that girl!"

"How do you mean?" I said.

"I told you Moira, didn't I? I said that Carly wouldn't give up. I've told Moira all of this," she said, looking at me and then my uncle. "Mind you, I never mentioned it to my Raymond. I didn't want to upset him."

"What?" I said, looking from her to Moira.

Moira looked away. She clearly didn't want to get involved in the conversation. I understood. It was her job, to be neutral and comforting at the same time.

"Raymond told you about how Kelly was afraid, scared, jumping out of her skin at the slightest thing?"

I nodded.

"She used to get these phone calls. I was never in when they came, neither was Raymond. We didn't know … you know, whether she was making them up or not. We thought it might have been one of

Vincent's friends. She always rang 1471 afterwards but she never got the number."

I remembered the phone calls. The deep breathing, the words *two-timer* over and over again.

"I got in one night after going out. My Kelly was in a terrible state. Someone had just that minute rung, she said. I tried to calm her down but she was hysterical. She took it all very bad, see. I picked up the phone and dialled 1471 just on the off chance that the person had forgotten to hold back their number."

She was quiet for a moment and I noticed Moira looking away, out of the window, miles away. She'd probably heard the story over and over.

"That speaking voice … it gave me a number. I pressed the redial and after a couple of rings a voice answered. The person said that I'd got through to the Stratford branch of McDonald's."

Mrs Ford looked at all of us with some triumph in her eyes; as though she'd won some sort of an argument.

"Carly Dickens made the phone calls?" I said.

"She did."

"Did you speak to her about it?"

"She denied it. What do you expect?"

"Did you go to the police?"

"Kelly wouldn't let me. We had no evidence. I wanted to but I thought it would upset everyone."

"Have you told them since?" Tony interrupted, "I mean, after Kelly was killed."

"I think I did. I'm sure I did. I don't know. I was in such a state of shock after Kelly died. It affected me so badly…"

Mrs Ford's voice started to crack again and Moira leaned over to her.

"I'm sorry," I said to Mrs Ford, "I didn't mean to upset you. Honestly I didn't."

Mrs Ford nodded. She looked relieved. Perhaps it had done her some good to get it all off her chest.

"I must be going Maureen. I've got a long drive," Moira said, lifting Mrs Ford's cup and saucer over to the coffee table.

The older woman struggled to get out of the chair. I held out my hand to help her up and she took it. Her arm felt thin and she hardly weighed anything at all. There was, underneath the perfume, a strong smell of spirits.

"I'll walk you downstairs," I said.

My uncle looked like he was breathing a sigh of relief.

"I'll tidy up," he said, lifting two pink wafer biscuits and sliding them into his mouth.

Out on the street I remembered one last thing I wanted to ask Mrs Ford. She wouldn't like it I knew, but I thought it might well be the last time I saw her. While Moira was walking ahead I put my hand on her arm and spoke quietly, full of politeness to avoid causing offence.

"Does Raymond drive a car, Mrs Ford?" I said.

It took a minute for my words to sink in. She looked as if she'd not heard me properly. I opened my mouth to repeat the question when she tutted loudly, throwing my hand off.

"Why can't you leave my Raymond out of this? No, he doesn't drive a car. Why should he drive a car? He doesn't own one. Is that enough for you?"

I looked hopelessly over in Moira's direction. Moira shrugged her shoulders and walked away towards the parked cars along the way. Mrs Ford gave me a look of daggers and followed her. The two of them were headed for a red hatchback car that was parked by a meter.

I stood and looked at it with disbelief. *A red hatchback car*. I walked on, overtaking Mrs Ford, and stood by the bonnet of the car looking awkward. Moira looked puzzled as if she expected me to say something. From behind her Mrs Ford's face was completely blank. I walked around the car looking for signs of the hit-and-run. As I was doing it I knew it was ridiculous. There were no marks on the bonnet and the tyres were coal black. It was in pristine condition.

Both women were standing staring at me.

"Is anything wrong?" Moira said.

I noticed then that Moira had a bunch of keys in her hand. It was her car. The woman from Victim Support.

"Nothing at all," I said, feeling foolish.

I stood on the pavement and watched them drive off. As I was standing there I counted two other red hatchbacks that passed by. How stupid of me. One of the most popular types of car in everyone's favourite colour.

A red hatchback. There were thousands of them.

When I got back into the office I heard the warble of my mobile phone. I had to dig deep into my bag to get it out. From the next room I could hear the tap tap tap of my uncle at his computer.

"Is that Patsy Kelly?" a male voice said.

"Speaking," I said, crisply.

"It's Liam Casey here."

"Hi," I said, quickly interested. I hadn't thought he'd phone.

"Are you there?" he said, his voice breaking up a bit.

I stood up and walked across to the window hoping to get a better line.

"I'm here, Liam. What can I do for you?"

"You asked me about the flat, the squat. Whether anyone knew about it."

"Yes?" I said.

"Carly knew about it. She came to see me once after we broke up. She wanted to talk about us getting back together. I brought her here to the flat. It was a long time ag … three, fo … months. I di … think ab … her when … asked."

The line was crackling badly and I was losing some of what Liam said.

"I can't quite hear you…" I raised my voice.

After that the line went dead. I shook my mobile in an irritated way. I would need to speak to Liam again.

I sat down feeling the tiniest bit excited. Carly knew that Liam lived in Huxley Point, yet she had lied about it when I'd spoken to her. Neither had she told the police, otherwise they would have most certainly brought Liam in for questioning.

There was a sum adding up in my head. Carly knew that Kelly was seeing Liam. Mrs Ford said that she made abusive phone calls to Kelly calling her a *two-timer*. When Kelly left home only Carly Dickens could have guessed where she might have gone.

I wondered how tight Carly's alibi was.

17

The Red Car

"If only we knew where Carly Dickens was when Kelly Ford fell off that building."

I looked hard at my uncle. We'd been talking about the case ever since Liam Casey's phone call. The main problem we had was a lack of information, all of which was in a file in the CID room.

My uncle had been a policeman for a long time before he became a private detective. I knew he had friends inside the police station. If he wanted to, he could find out things that he wasn't supposed to know.

"If I just knew about her alibi I'd feel more confident about taking this to Des Murray."

"OK," he said, standing up and stretching his arms, "you've made your point. I'll go and see if any of the lads are in the pub. A couple of them owe me a favour or two."

I couldn't believe how helpful my uncle was being. I stood for a moment watching him and waiting for some condition to be attached to the visit. He took a small mirror out of his drawer and looked at himself for a moment. Then he used a clothes brush on his suit jacket. As he walked out of the office door he was humming to himself.

Then I got it. He was enjoying himself. After months of sitting in front of the new computer he was being given a reason to go and see his old mates. He was finally getting tired of his Virtual Life and he wanted to edge back into the real world. I don't know if that fact pleased me or not. All the same, I was glad that he was going to help me.

I looked at my watch. It was nearly three o'clock. I hadn't heard from Joey and I wondered if he'd had any luck following Raymond and finding the red car. I pushed down a feeling of heaviness in my stomach when I thought of Joey Hooper. Was he, at that very moment, thinking about our kisses the night before? Seeing the two of us as a couple? I was going to have to call a halt to it, tell him that it couldn't go any further. It gave me a bad feeling; like I'd given a present to someone and now, a day later, I was going to take it back.

Weariness hit me. Everything was only half-done. The case had a couple of leads but other things needed to be checked and verified. I felt bogged down by all the things I had to do. Why wasn't life ever straightforward and simple?

I made myself clear my desk up, putting pens and bits of paper away, filing documents and disks and sorting out some bills and receipts. I immediately felt better, as if by doing it I was tidying up the complications of my day-to-day life. I pushed everything out of my head and took out two clean sheets of paper. At the top of one I wrote RED CAR and at the top of the other I wrote CARLY DICKENS. Then I proceeded to fill in everything I knew about each of them.

When I'd finished I looked from one to the other.

At first, when Carly Dickens had been run over, I'd thought that she and Kelly had been targeted by the same person, perhaps Raymond Ford. He was obsessive about his sister and had tried to kill Carly because of something she knew. Until the red car was found I couldn't be sure about it.

Over the last day or so the evidence had started to turn in another direction. It had formed into a giant arrow and was pointing at Carly Dickens. She had lost Liam Casey and then he had taken up with Kelly. Carly had made the abusive phone calls and she must have worked out where Kelly was staying that last week.

I sat back in my chair and looked at the page that said RED CAR at the top. One of the things I'd written underneath was HIT-AND-RUN? What if it had been something as simple as that? A genuine accident in which the driver had got scared and driven off.

Then there was the red car in Raymond Ford's garage. It was there when I'd looked in the afternoon but gone later that night.

What if the garage I'd looked in wasn't Raymond Ford's at all? If I'd never seen the red car in what I'd thought was Raymond's garage, then how different it would make everything look. I took my pen and idly drew a line across the page.

That would leave Carly as the possible murderer and the hit-and-run as just that, an unconnected crime.

Maybe there was not and never had been a red car in Raymond's garage.

I was distracted from my thoughts by heavy footsteps coming up the stairs to the office. In a second the door flew open and Joey Hooper stood there. He was wearing jeans and a shirt that hung outside. In spite of my worries about seeing him I couldn't help but smile. His face was glowing and he had the kind of expression that suggested he'd just won a lot of money.

"So this is where you work!" he said, rubbing his hands together.

"Yes, this is the Nerve Centre," I said, stretching back in the chair, pushing my bits of paper away from me. "What are you so pleased about?"

He sat on the other side of my desk, his eyes looking around the room, finally resting on my desk. He picked up the bit of paper on which I'd written RED CAR and crossed it through.

"I've been a good boy," he said, delightedly.

He looked straight at me and I couldn't help but grin back. He was talking about the case, I knew, but part of me thought that he was referring to the previous evening.

"I followed Raymond," he said, "all the way down to the river. You know the factories down there? The ones that closed years ago?"

I nodded. I'd recently been involved in a double murder down by the River Lea. It wasn't a happy memory.

"Some of the buildings have been converted into small workshops now. Woodwork, kitchen tiles, car mechanics."

I shook my head, not sure where he was going.

"Look, I'll start at the beginning. Raymond went out about lunch-time and I followed from a distance. He looked around a few times; he was worried, I could tell. He obviously didn't want anyone to know where he was going. I'm good at following people, see. You'll probably remember that."

I did remember. When I'd first met Joey he'd spent a lot of his time following one of the men who'd killed his brother. I, on the other hand, wasn't terribly good at following people.

"He took me down to the river and we walked around the houses a bit. Literally, up one street, down the next. I was getting into my stride when he suddenly stopped. I walked past him, on round the corner and when I looked back he was opening the door to a red hatchback."

I didn't say anything at first. I was almost disappointed. After making a good argument for the car not existing it was a blow to have it back on the scene.

"I thought you'd be pleased," Joey said.

"I am, I am," I said, giving Joey's arm a squeeze.

But it made me feel weary again and I knew I had to bring Raymond Ford back into the picture.

Later, in a local pizza restaurant, Joey went through the whole story again. This time I asked him questions every few minutes and jotted down anything that I thought was important.

"He got in the car and sat there for a few minutes. I stood watching from round the corner. I wasn't exactly in the position to follow him if he moved off."

I laughed at that and imagined Joey running down the street after the red hatchback. After giving me a look of extreme tolerance, he continued.

"He pulled out slowly and did a three point turn. Then he drove about twenty metres down the street and turned into one of the old factories. A place that's now full of small workshops. I walked up and looked at the sign outside. There's three car repair places, a couple of specialist garages and a company that takes cars for scrap. You know, removes all the working bits and then compresses the rest."

I did know. It was the kind of place that Billy often used to go to.

"You didn't go in?"

"Nope. I'd pushed my luck far enough. I didn't want to bump into him. I'm going to go back in the morning and find out which place he's put the car into. Then I'll ring you and we can decide what to do."

He sat silently for a minute. He'd given me all his information and now he didn't know what to say. I pushed a piece of garlic bread towards him and he shook his head, his breathing quick, as though he'd just been running.

"What about you? What have you found out?"

I told him about Liam's phone call and he was as surprised as I had been. Liam had been the last person we'd expected help from. I also mentioned Mrs Ford's visit and her story about the anonymous phone calls.

He listened and grew quieter as I spoke. I knew, as I was talking, that I would have to get round to the subject of the previous evening. While I was dragging out the story about Carly Dickens I was already forming the words in my head. *I'm sorry Joey, but I'm still with Billy*, or *Joey, there's no room in my life for a relationship with you*. Even as the words joined up to make sentences I was already feeling embarrassed by them.

"Patsy," Joey said, as soon as I stopped talking.

"Yes?"

It was as if he'd not been listening to what I'd been saying; as if he, like me, had been thinking of another subject.

"About last night. It was great you know, but I'm not really ready for stuff like that yet. It's such a short time since Paul died and I've only just come out of the nick. It's just too soon."

I must have been sitting with my mouth open wide because he began to look worried.

"It's nothing to do with you. I think you're great. It's just that, at the moment, I'm not up to getting involved. Do you understand?"

He put his hand on top of mine. I looked down at it. His black skin criss-crossing my white fingers. He was telling me that it wasn't going any further, that he wasn't ready for it.

"That's OK," I said, "I understand. That's fine."

I should have been pleased, but I wasn't.

Don't get me wrong. It was what I wanted; it got me out of a difficult situation. It meant that I could put the other night down to a momentary error of judgement and start to feel good about my letter from Billy. I couldn't help but feel deflated though. As though I'd been full to bursting and now I was shapeless and empty. I spent the rest of the meal chewing endlessly at the pizza and keeping a frozen smile on my face.

When we left the restaurant he gave me a peck on the cheek. A friendship kiss. It was what I wanted – to put things back the way they'd been before we'd kissed. Why on earth wasn't I happy about it?

When I got home my mum and Gerry were out. The place was strangely quiet and I sat down on the stairs dumping my shoulder bag on the floor. The phone rang and I almost couldn't be bothered to pick it up. I forced myself and heard my uncle's voice amidst a babble of background noise and music.

"One of my mates went into the files and looked up the notes on the Dickens girl. Not being a suspect she was never asked for a precise alibi. She does say that she finished work and went shopping afterwards."

"Right," I said, dully.

Where did that leave us then?

"Des Murray came in about half-an-hour ago and says he wants to see you in the morning. I told him you're not very well but I'll bring you in later."

"OK," I said.

Did I really care? Wouldn't it be just as well to hand it all over to him now? The suspicions, the inaccuracies? The red car?

I realized that the phone had gone dead. My uncle must have said goodbye and hung up. I slammed the receiver down and went upstairs to bed.

18

Arrested

After an uneasy night I went into the office. My uncle wasn't in yet and I wondered if he'd had a late night out drinking with his old friends. The place was surprisingly quiet without him. All I could hear was the sound of the traffic outside; no tapping from his keyboard, no humming songs, no sound of the kettle boiling up never-ending cups of tea or coffee.

Truthfully the office seemed a lonely place without him. Even though he drove me mad at times, he was company of sorts. His presence often stopped me brooding about things, made me get to work, be positive.

I made an effort to push all thoughts of Billy and Joey Hooper out of my mind and think about the case again. At that moment there were two possible solutions and neither of them was totally satisfactory.

Raymond loved his half-sister too much; he followed her and slept with her clothes under his pillow. Could it be that he had taken it further? Had Raymond tried to be more than a brother to his sister? Kelly had moved out, Liam had said that *Kelly was desperate to get away from him.* Perhaps he had approached her; tried to kiss her or touch her. She had left in a panic and Raymond, afraid that she might say something, had found her and silenced her.

Had he tried to run over Carly because he thought that Kelly had told her? If so, how had Raymond known that Kelly was staying at Huxley Point? The only person who knew about that was Carly Dickens.

I sat up suddenly. What if Raymond had gone to Carly for help?

Carly was angry at Kelly for having Liam; she had made nasty phone calls in order to upset her ex-friend. She might have sympathized with Raymond, led him on, told him where Kelly was, told him that Kelly had told her things that Raymond had done. She might have pushed Raymond to commit the murder.

I found myself grabbing a bit of paper and writing it down. It explained a lot. It certainly gave Raymond a reason to run Carly over and try to kill her. She knew too much.

If only I knew more about Raymond and his sister. That was the key to it, I was sure. The one person who could tell me the most was Maureen Ford, their mother.

I looked at my mobile phone. It was nine o'clock. Should I ring her? See if she would speak to me? I remembered her sitting grumpily in the red hatch-back, being driven away by the woman from Victim Support. She was so defensive whenever I mentioned Raymond's name. Maybe that was because she knew more than she was saying.

The office phone rang suddenly, making me jump. I went to pick it up thinking it might be Joey with news of the red car. Then I remembered that Joey usually rang the mobile. I let the answerphone pick the message up, listening in case it was important. I heard a male voice.

"This is Des Murray. It's my umpteenth phone call for Patsy Kelly. If she doesn't come into the station in the next hour, she'll be sorry."

That was it. I looked at the phone in an affronted way. Was he threatening me? I'd agreed to go in later on. Wasn't that enough for him?

I went back to thinking about Maureen Ford, trying to work out a good argument for her speaking to me. She was obviously hostile. If only I could get someone to speak to her on my behalf. And then it came to me. Moira, the woman from Victim Support. She had spent a lot of time with Mrs Ford;

she seemed to have become a friend of sorts. She was part of an organization which was linked to the police. She should be the very person who would see my point of view.

I got the office phone book out and looked up the number of the local Victim Support Coordinator. A woman answered.

"Stratford Victim Support. May I help you?"

"Good morning. I'm trying to get in touch with one of your colleagues. She's working with a client who is involved in an ongoing investigation. I only have her first name. Moira."

I spoke quickly, expecting them to be awkward. I wasn't disappointed.

"And you are?" The woman said it crisply.

"I work for Anthony Hamer Investigations and we're following up a case…"

"I'm sorry we don't give information out to agencies other than the police."

"Could I just leave a message for Moira? Then she could either ring me or not. That way you're not actually giving me any information?"

I raised my voice at the end even though it wasn't actually a question. It was a polite way of making her think she was in charge. Which of course she was.

"I can do that, of course," she said, and I smiled. "Who was it you wanted to get in touch with?"

"Her name's Moira…"

"That's odd," the woman said, "we don't have anyone called Moira working for us."

"Oh," I said.

"Although I have been away from the office for a couple of weeks. It could be that we were stretched and had to pass the work on to one of the other areas; Tower Hamlets, Leytonstone, Walthamstow. Somewhere like that. You could try them. Here, I'll give you the numbers."

I took the numbers down and thanked the woman, who had, after all, turned out to be helpful.

It didn't take long to ring the three numbers. None of them had a Moira working for them. I was puzzled. A man from the Walthamstow Support Group said he would ask around and see if Moira was a freelance. That sometimes happened, he said; professional counsellors often did some unpaid work when certain cases interested them. I gave him the office number as well as my mobile.

There was no more I could do. It was ten-past-ten and there was no sign of my uncle. Perhaps he had a bad hangover. I decided to write to Billy. I turned the computer on and opened up a file. I called it BILLYLET and started to type.

Dear Billy, I typed, *I just got your letter. I've missed you lots.*

I went on like that for a few lines saying how much I cared for him and how I wished I was there with him. Then I sat back and read it over. The word *Love* stood out awkwardly as if it didn't belong there. I let my finger hover over the delete button. It sounded sickly somehow and not believable. I pushed the button and watched the computer eat up the letters.

I went back to the beginning and started again. This time I wrote about the case and what I was doing. I even mentioned, in passing, that I'd met Joey Hooper again.

I was distracted then by a police siren that had come along the road and seemed to have stopped outside the office. The noise of it was deafening. I walked over to the window to see it parked at an angle, its light still turning frantically even though the siren itself had stopped. I was wondering what had happened when I heard heavy footsteps coming up the stairs. The office door opened and two male officers came into the room. One of them was old enough to be my father; the other looked like he'd only just left school.

"Patricia Kelly?" one of them said.

I nodded, shocked at their presence. My first thought was that something had happened to my mum. This disappeared though when I noted their cocky stance, the older one looking round the office with a barely disguised grin on his face, the younger one looking me up and down with relish.

"Inspector Murray would like you to help him with his enquiries," he said, eyeing the older man.

"Is this necessary?" I said, a feeling of embarrassment creeping up my neck.

"If you refuse to come we'll be forced to arrest you."

"On what charge?" I demanded.

"Perverting the course of justice," the older one said, a smile from ear to ear.

"Withholding evidence in a major investigation," the younger one said, removing his baton from his belt.

It was a joke. It had to be. Des Murray was making a point. I walked over to my computer and saved the letter to Billy. Then I picked up my bag and the office keys.

"OK boys. It's a fair cop. Please don't beat me up in the cells."

I said it all in a bored voice and stood with my hands in mid-air as though they were pointing guns at me. The younger one looked puzzled, then irritated. The older one cleared his throat a couple of times and held the door open.

"Just doing our job, Miss Kelly. This way, if you please."

Des Murray was waiting for me in the interview room. He was smoking a cigarette and sharing a joke with a female officer.

"Am I under arrest?" I said, sitting down with a thump.

"It could be arranged," he said.

"Haven't you got something better to do than harass innocent members of the public?" I demanded.

"What were you doing driving Carly Dickens home on the night that she was run over? Why didn't you come into the station as you were asked to do?"

His voice had risen and I crossed my legs and folded my arms in annoyance. What right had he got to treat me in such a way?

"What have you got to say?"

I swallowed a couple of times, not sure of what to do. I should apologize, I knew that. I'd been in the wrong, not coming into the station and telling them everything I knew. If Heather Warren had been at work I would have done it immediately. But the truth was I couldn't stand Des Murray with his patronizing ways. I looked at the tape recorder machine that was on the table. It had no tape in it – it wasn't even a proper interview.

"I have the right to remain silent," I said, calmly.

Des Murray looked at me with pure malice.

"OK Miss Kelly. I'll tell you what we'll do. You can go with this officer now to one of our cells while I continue with my enquiries. Should you change your mind while in that cell and decide that you want to speak to me, the officer on duty will contact me by radio. I'll try to get back and see you as soon as possible but it could be some time. Five, six hours, whatever."

He was walking towards the door of the room,.

The WPC stood up and smoothed her skirt down. He meant it. A feeling of panic grabbed my insides. I'd gone too far.

"I'm sorry, I'm sorry. Of course I'll speak to you."

I stood up, my hands in mid-air again.

"I was coming to see you today anyway. Honestly Des. The only reason I waited this long was because I was going to bring you something concrete. I was just angry about being brought in by car. That's all. I'll tell you everything. Honestly Des. Everything."

I was grovelling as hard as I could.

Des Murray stopped walking and turned round. He made a signal to the WPC and she pulled her chair over to the table and got a pen and pad out of a drawer.

"I want everything that you know. Don't leave a single thing out, do you understand me?"

I nodded weakly.

"And don't call me Des. It's Mr Murray to you," he added, pulling a cigarette out of a packet.

I started at the beginning, meekly emphasizing how I'd been drawn into the case against my will. I told him about the stuff I'd brought from Heather, the cassette tape from Raymond Ford. I reminded him how he'd said that the case had been put on a back burner and that he was no longer considering murder but suicide.

I described the night of the accident and the red car. I hadn't been the only one to see the red car, I'd said, that was why I'd not rushed into the police station.

All the while he sat and listened without expression, smoking one cigarette after another. At times he seemed to deliberately blow the smoke in my direction. The WPC was quietly taking notes. Every now and then she used the top end of her pen to scratch a place behind her ear.

Des Murray became more interested when I told him about the hidden flat in Huxley Point, and about Liam Casey being Kelly's secret boyfriend. I noticed the WPC underlining what she was writing. It was obviously new information for them. I added the details about Carly Dickens' nuisance phone calls and her knowledge of Liam's flat.

Then I told him about seeing the red hatchback in Raymond's garage and how Raymond had gone to great lengths to hide it.

"Why didn't you come to us as soon as you saw the red car?" Des Murray said, squashing his cigarette in the ashtray. "Even you must have known how important that was. It could have opened the whole case up."

His voice was full of contempt. He was right, although it wasn't fair that I should take all the blame. If he wasn't such a total pig to deal with I might feel more confident going to him with information that might turn out to be a waste of time. Why couldn't he see that?

A warbling sound came from my pocket and I

looked over at him to see if it was OK for me to answer the mobile. It was Joey Hooper, breathless and excited.

"I've found the car. It's in that place I told you about. It's called BIG FRANK'S PARTS. The owner says a young lad sold it to him yesterday for almost nothing. He signed the sales docket *Ray Smith*. Imaginative or not?"

"Is it still in one piece?" I said and mouthed *red hatchback* to Des Murray.

"Just. It's due to go in the crusher in about an hour. The manager took some persuading but I think he'll hold it."

"Are there any marks on it?" I said, my fingers crossed, hoping that it was the car that tried to run over Carly Dickens.

"Dent on the bonnet. Stress marks on the front tyres."

"I'm coming now and I'm bringing the police with me," I said, pressing the *call over* button.

Des Murray looked fit to burst.

"You've found the red car! Where is it, Patsy? Don't muck me about."

"It's in a scrapyard down by the river."

He turned without a word and walked towards the door. I grabbed my bag and followed him.

"And don't call me Patsy. It's Miss Kelly to you."

He laughed out loud, all the way along the corridor and into a squad car.

19
Evidence

When we arrived at BIG FRANK'S PARTS Joey was standing outside talking to a large man who was wearing dark blue overalls. Des Murray leaped out of the car and hurried towards them as though a murder was about to happen at that very moment. I followed more sedately, closing the car door that he had left open.

"Inspector Murray, local CID. I understand you have a suspicious motor vehicle on your premises?"

I caught Joey's glance and rolled my eyes. Why couldn't Des just use plain English? Big Frank was looking worried.

"It weren't nothing to do with me Inspector. I'm clean, I am. I don't take bent gear. I learned my lesson…"

All the while the huge man was rubbing his hands up and down his stomach as though covering up something that was there. Joey was looking mildly bemused. I noticed Des Murray looking at him.

"Don't I know you?" he said to Joey.

Then I remembered. It had been Des Murray who had actually arrested Joey some months before. Joey was looking uncomfortable, his hands in his pockets. He deliberately looked away from Des. I butted in.

"We're wasting time. Shouldn't we look at the hatchback?"

"It's over here, Inspector." Big Frank said. "The lad said he couldn't afford to keep it any longer. It's a bit of an old banger, see. I was doing him a favour. It was all straight and above board. I learned my lesson, see…"

"What did the lad look like?"

"Well now," Big Frank said and started to rub his chin. "He was quite thin, I remember. Brownish hair, I think. Tallish, sort of round shoulders. Looked as though he had the troubles of the world on his back. Didn't look like no car thief to me. I know, see, because I've been in the business a while."

"You've got a registration document, I take it?" Des Murray said, looking bored.

"Now look, Inspector, the boy said he'd mislaid it. It's an old car. I only gave him twenty smackers for it."

Des Murray tutted loudly and walked off in the

direction that Big Frank was pointing. The car was parked round the back of the reception offices. It sat alongside the shells of three other cars. Their insides had been picked dry; the seats, the steering wheels, the mirrors and the tyres, all gone. Two of them had their bonnets up and the engines sitting on the ground beside them. This was what should have happened to Raymond Ford's car.

"My boy was just about to start on this car, see, when this young man turns up and tells me that it might have been in an accident. I stops, right away. I always cooperate with the police, see. Ever since that trouble a couple of years ago…"

The bonnet had a dent on it and the front tyres had lost a lot of rubber.

"Will you be able to prove that it was the car that hit Carly Dickens?" I said.

"Not easily, no. It could have been washed; it could have been driven a lot since the night it happened. Course, if we'd known earlier…"

Des Murray's nostrils flared but I ignored him. If it hadn't been for me and Joey the red car would be in the crusher by now.

"The fact that he tried to get rid of the car in such a secretive way must help?" I said.

"Um," Des Murray conceded.

I remembered then that his mother had tried to cover up for him.

"Mrs Ford said he didn't even own a car!"

"Maybe he didn't. Possibly it's a *stolen* car," Des Murray said, looking hard at Big Frank.

"I shouldn't think so, Inspector. I don't take stolen cars. What lad is going to steal a car like this and then get twenty quid for it?"

Des Murray took a small radio out of his pocket and spoke rapidly into it.

"Delta two four, Inspector Murray. I'm down at a scrapyard at the Leaside Trading Estate. I need a vehicle carrier to do a pick-up ASAP. Also could you do a registration check. I want the name of the current owner of a red Peugeot 205 hatchback..."

He talked on, reading out the registration number into the radio. Big Frank had both his hands in his pockets and was looking stressed. He started to talk to Joey in a low voice. I could just hear him.

"Just doing the boy a favour ... what's wrong with that...? Who'd steal such an old banger? Too much paperwork these days... I've been clean now for over three years..."

I heard Des Murray's radio crackle and saw him turn away to listen to what was being said. I looked at the car and remembered it reversing towards me, coming at me down the dark wet road. I'd stood back, afraid that it would hit me, and then I'd found out about the hit-and-run. Had it been Raymond?

Des Murray turned back towards us.

"It wasn't Raymond Ford's car at all," he said, looking at Big Frank, then Joey, then me.

"It was stolen?" I said.

If Raymond had stolen the car it would explain why his mother was so sure that he didn't drive.

"Nope. It wasn't stolen. It was registered in the name of Maureen Ford."

"There you are!" said Big Frank looking pleased with himself. "I said the boy was honest, didn't I?"

None of us spoke.

Raymond had driven his mother's car to run Carly over.

20

Policework

Raymond Ford was arrested the next day. He was brought into the police station with his mother, and he refused to answer any questions. His mother was distraught and kept accusing the police of having a vendetta against her son.

After a few hours he was charged with the attempted murder of Carly Dickens. He said nothing when the charge was read to him.

I knew all this because my uncle had been into the station on another matter and had found out the details of what was happening. He had come back into the office bursting with information.

"Didn't they charge him with Kelly's murder?" I said.

"No. His mother swears he was with her."

"Then what reason could he have for trying to murder Carly? It doesn't fit!" I said, frustrated.

"They've also interviewed Carly Dickens. She admits to making the phone calls but denies having anything to do with Kelly Ford's death. Her alibi's vague but there's absolutely no other evidence to link her to Huxley Point."

"Oh," I said.

"Don't look so miserable. If it hadn't been for you they'd never have found that car."

"It wasn't me, it was Joey Hooper." I said and then looked reproachfully at the phone.

After Des Murray had left BIG FRANK'S Joey and me stayed with the red car until the police tow truck arrived. We watched it being taken away and both smiled with satisfaction. Something had gone right. Raymond Ford had been seen trying to get rid of a car that in all probability had been in a hit-and-run.

Des Murray was pleased. Big Frank wasn't.

"I'm out of pocket, twenty quid. That's what you get for trying to help someone. I'm too trusting for my own good," he'd said, shaking his head.

We left him there and walked off. My car was still at the office and Joey was going home to get on with his studying. His A levels were looming up. At the bus stop we had to go our separate ways.

"Joey, I can't thank you enough," I'd said.

"I enjoyed it," he said as his bus appeared round the corner.

I looked at the bus approaching and realized, with panic, that I didn't have a reason to see him again. I tried to think of something to say: *Why don't we go to the cinema at the weekend? Do you fancy going up West to a club?* Instead I found myself talking about the case.

"I'm hoping they charge Raymond with Kelly's murder. Then the case will be closed," I said, the bus screeching to a halt beside us.

"I'll ring you," he said, getting on.

As the bus disappeared down the road I felt strangely lost. A little bit of me had wanted him to hug or kiss me. Just for friendship's sake, I told myself. Instead he had just leaped on the bus and gone to his seat with hardly a wave.

Was that it between Joey and me?

I gave up waiting for my bus about ten seconds later and started a long, lonely walk through the back streets towards the office. It was probably for the best, I told myself; being friends with Joey might be very confusing. And it was only eleven months and just over a week until Billy came back.

"That reminds me –" my uncle was still talking about the flurry of activity at the police station – "Des Murray wants you to go in and make a statement about seeing the car in Raymond's garage. He also wants … what's his name?"

"Joey?" I said.

"That's it. He wants him to make a statement about following Raymond and seeing him deliver the car to the scrap merchant's. He said to tell you to get down there this afternoon or he'd send someone out to get you."

"There's no need for that," I said, smiling.

I picked up the office phone and dialled Joey's number. It was work, I told myself, nothing more. Afterwards I went into the toilet and spent more time than I should have fixing my hair and putting some lipstick on.

Just as I was leaving the office the phone rang.

"I'm calling from Walthamstow Victim Support. Am I speaking to Patsy Kelly?" It was a man's voice. I remembered then my enquiries about Moira, the woman who was always with Mrs Ford.

"Yes," I said.

"You asked us about a worker called Moira. I'm afraid I've had no luck tracing this woman. It's a pretty unusual name these days, Moira."

"Yes, it is," I said, eager to get going. "Well, thanks anyway."

The man wanted to talk though. He'd gone to some trouble for me. It was the least I could do to listen.

"I went through all our records for a couple of years back but we've never had a Moira working as a support worker. I've tried all the freelances as well."

"Thanks ever so much for your trouble."

"The only Moira I've come across in the last couple of years was a client, about six months ago. A *young* woman as well. Other than that I'm afraid you'll have to try some other area."

"I will," I said. "Thanks a lot."

I didn't bother to write it down. Now that everything had come out into the open it was up to Des Murray to try and get information out of Mrs Ford. It wasn't my problem any more.

Des Murray put both me and Joey in his office and asked us to write out a statement explaining what had happened. He gave Joey a long look as if he was trying to place him. Joey just stared back insolently until Des Murray looked away.

It was an awkward moment. When Des Murray left Joey looked ill at ease. He kept shifting his position on the chair, looking around out of the window at the rest of the CID officers working outside.

"We can do this in a hour," I said, "then we can go."

He nodded, clearing his throat. I made a space on the desk and he sat on one side while I sat on the other. After a few minutes writing he seemed to relax and we seemed like a couple of students taking an exam. From time to time I looked up to see him concentrating. Then I looked back to my own bit of paper and made myself think about all the details of the afternoon when I'd seen the red car in Raymond's garage.

After about twenty minutes a uniformed officer brought in two polystyrene cups of coffee.

"Inspector Murray's been called out. He asked me to thank you for all the trouble you've gone to and says he'll let you know how the case progresses."

"Are we talking about *the* Inspector Murray?" I said.

The man smiled wryly and left us there. I drank my coffee while finishing the statement. Joey was taking longer, his handwriting looking a lot neater than mine. Should I redraft it? I wondered. I didn't want Des Murray taking the mickey out of it behind my back. I decided against it. It was altogether too much effort.

I glanced at a couple of box files that were on the floor behind Des Murray's chair. It was the stuff I'd brought from Heather's flat. I picked up one and opened it, immediately recognizing the two videos and the piles of statements and notes and interviews that had come from the two-week investigation into Kelly Ford's death.

Judging by the amount of paperwork, it looked like the police had interviewed hundreds of people. And after all that the killer was probably someone very close to Kelly, with a good reason to kill her.

If Raymond Ford had killed his sister, he wasn't saying. He wasn't even admitting to the hit-and-run even though there was compelling evidence to link him to it. Carly Dickens had a motive and she'd known where Kelly was, but she was denying having anything to do with the murder.

Who killed Kelly Ford? Who stood on the top of that building and pushed her off?

I flicked through the files and saw the name Vincent Black. Vince had good reason to be heart-broken, angry, even furious at Kelly but he didn't have the means. He couldn't reach out from prison and have his ex-girlfriend killed. There was Liam, his righthand man; but Liam had fallen in love with Kelly.

Underneath the notes about Vincent Black were the details of the death of Dan Mackenzie.

I sat back, my eyes scanning over the stuff about the attack in the jeweller's. I'd read it before but a grim fact had occurred to me. Dan Mackenzie's death had been the beginning of a downward spiral of events. Of the four young people in that shop, two were dead, one badly injured and the other in prison.

Further down the page there was a cutting from a local weekly newspaper. As I was reading it I could hear Joey moving about as if he'd finished what he was doing.

Dan Mackenzie, only son of John and Nicola Mackenzie, was only twenty-five when a blow from a young thug ended his life. An Honours graduate, Dan and his long-term girlfriend had plans to do voluntary work for a year in Africa…

I stopped there amid a rush of emotions. In a

second Billy's face came into my head and I felt this prod of guilt. Joey looked up and gave me a smile.

"Finished?" he said.

"Yeah, just let me read this," I said, avoiding eye contact with him.

Yesterday, his killer, an unemployed petty criminal, eighteen-year-old Vincent Black, was imprisoned for twelve months for Assault. Is this justice?

I read on. It was full of details about the assault on Dan Mackenzie and strong arguments for longer prison sentences. The young man had apparently gone to the jeweller's to pick up something for his girlfriend. Underneath was a snapshot of the two of them. I glanced at it, then looked at the caption. *Dan Mackenzie and his girlfriend, Moira Henderson.*

Something jarred with me and I looked back over the article and at the photograph. The woman looked familiar. Her face was thin and her hair was cropped tightly into her head. Her name was *Moira Henderson*.

"What is it?" Joey said.

I didn't answer. I took my glasses off and gave them a rapid clean. Then I looked hard at the photo.

"Moira Henderson," I said out loud.

"Who?"

I began to feel excited.

"The woman who is always with Mrs Ford, the young woman who said she was from Victim Support."

"What about her."

"I think she was Dan Mackenzie's girlfriend!"

Joey looked at me, puzzled.

"None of the Victim Support agencies around here have a *Moira* working for them. I tried them all. Walthamstow office rang me this morning and said that the only Moira that they'd come into contact with was a client, about six months ago."

I handed the article over to Joey, pointing with my finger to the section.

"You think this is the same woman?" he said, puzzled. "Why would she be helping Mrs Ford?"

"She had a red car as well," I said, remembering the polished, well-looked-after hatchback that I'd seen.

"But we've got the car," Joey said. "We know which car it was."

"But have we got the driver?" I said, a fantastic story starting to build up in my head.

"You've lost me," Joey said, standing up, stretching his arms up as though he were about to do some exercises.

"Dan Mackenzie is killed from the blow in the jeweller's. The video of which was shown in court as evidence, right?"

Joey shrugged his shoulders.

"In that video both girls, Kelly and Carly, stand by while Dan Mackenzie is beaten up. I saw it. They actually looked impressed by it all. Imagine his girlfriend, Moira, watching that video in court. How she must have hated those girls!"

"So she killed Kelly?" Joey said it with a look of incredulity.

"Why not? She bides her time, follows her. Remember Kelly said she was being followed by a red car. Moira has a red car!"

"Then afterwards she befriends the mother and brother?"

"And uses Mrs Ford's car to run over Carly. That way she throws everyone off the scent."

"Then why does Raymond get rid of it?"

That stopped me. I didn't know. I sat back with all the bits of paper from the file on my lap. Perhaps I was wrong. More than likely Raymond Ford was confessing to it all at that very moment.

I flicked through the documents in the box file and then packed it all away and picked up the other one. When I got near the bottom I found what I wanted. A data sheet on Dan Mackenzie, his parents, his close friends. There at the bottom was Moira's name and address. She lived in Walthamstow.

"This is a loose end Joey. I've got to go and see her," I said. "Are you coming?"

Joey gave me a slow look. It said a lot of things, like, *Enough Patsy, give it up now, you could be wrong*. After a few seconds he nodded his head.

I was grateful for the company.

21

Afternoon Tea

It didn't take us long to get to Walthamstow. Joey held the A–Z and navigated. Moira lived in the Village area in a terraced Victorian house. The streets were narrow and quiet with speed humps every few metres. There were trees along the pavement and small, neat front gardens.

We knocked on the door not knowing what to expect. The truth was I didn't even know what I was going to say to the woman. I needed to know if Dan Mackenzie had been her boyfriend. I also needed to know why she was always with Mrs Ford and why she was claiming to be from Victim Support.

The last thing I was going to do was accuse her of murder. Joey Hooper looked mightily relieved when I told him.

The front door opened and a small, thin face looked out.

"Why don't you come in?" she said.

There was no surprise, no questions as to who we were and why we were there. She recognized me straight away. It was almost as if she was *expecting* me.

"Come into the kitchen," she called as we followed her up a tiny hallway.

The kitchen was small, with open shelving instead of cupboards and exposed brick walls instead of wallpaper. There were dishes and bowls displayed everywhere and bunches of dried herbs hanging upside down from the ceiling. An old wooden table sat in the middle with four odd chairs around it. Moira filled up a kettle and put it on top of an old-fashioned cooker.

It was like stepping back into the past.

"I'm just about to make afternoon tea. You can join me," Moira said, getting some tiny china cups and saucers off the shelves.

She seemed very calm. She laid each saucer down and then added the cups. She even took a small jug and sugar bowl out.

"I've made a carrot cake. Would you like some?"

"No thanks," I said, ill at ease with the normality of the scene.

"It was Dan's favourite. Carrot cake. He said I made the best carrot cake he'd ever tasted. The secret is to keep it moist, you see."

She stopped speaking and seemed to grip the edge of the table.

"Are you all right?" I said, standing up.

"Goodness, yes. It's been over eight months now since Dan died."

"I'm sorry," I said, not really knowing what to say.

"Why should you be sorry? You didn't know him. I'm the one who's sorry." She said it softly. "One day at a time. That's how I'm handling it. Two hundred of them; all on my own. All because some flash little nobody wanted to show off in front of a couple of girls."

She plonked down on to one of the chairs. I looked behind her and saw steam clouds coming out of the kettle. I gestured to Joey.

"I'll make the tea," he said, looking glad to have something to do.

"Are you all right?" I said again.

She wasn't crying. That was what was so strange. There was no redness in her face, no sense that she was even fighting the tears away. Her eyes were sharp and bright and her fists were balled up.

"I've had so much anger in me," she said. "So much hate."

Joey was pouring the tea into the china cups, trying not to react to what Moira was saying. I couldn't ignore it any longer.

"Moira, did you kill Kelly Ford?"

She looked at me and thought hard for a moment. Then she got up and went to a drawer and pulled out a padded envelope.

"My statement is in here," she said. "It's been ready ever since it happened. I've just been waiting for someone to come round."

She looked at Joey and then at the steaming cups of tea. She picked up a tray and placed the cups one by one on it and moved off. We followed her.

"Why don't we go into the living room?" she said as though we were just friends on a visit.

It was a small room with wooden floorboards and a giant settee that took up one wall. Above it there were a dozen or so clip frames, all with pictures of a young man of about twenty five. In some of the pictures he was with Moira. In others he was on his own or with friends. A couple looked like they were taken in other parts of the world; Africa or South America and somewhere very cold and snowy.

"Why don't you tell us what happened?" I said.

She handed me and Joey a cup of tea and then sat on the floor opposite us.

"I had a lot of help when Dan was killed. A lot of people visiting. Every day someone new called by to see if I was all right. By the time the trial came it had dropped off a bit. That was all right. I didn't expect to be mollycoddled for ever."

"That was in January?" I said.

"The trial was much harder than I'd thought it would be. The policeman in charge of the case told me not to go. He said it would upset me too much. But I wanted to face up to the lad who had taken Dan away from me."

"You saw the videos?"

She looked at me with surprise.

"Yes, I did. And I saw that young man smirking and grinning at his girlfriend whenever he could. It's something I'll never forget as long as I live."

"Is that why you started to follow Kelly? You did follow her around, didn't you?"

She looked annoyed for a moment.

"It's not as cut and dried as that," she said wearily.

"Why don't you let her tell it, Patsy?" Joey said, making a face at me.

"However much anger I felt, once the trial was over I tried to get on with my life. And I wasn't doing too badly until the middle of April, when a letter came through the door addressed to Dan and me. It was from the charity that we were going to go abroad with. They didn't know you see; no one had told them that he'd died. I just hadn't thought."

Her look of composure was unravelling and she began rubbing her neck with her hand.

"In the middle of April I just fell apart. It was as if it had only just happened again. I found myself going along to the shopping centre and sitting outside the jeweller's. Just watching. Day after day. That's when I saw her coming out with her new boyfriend."

"You mean Kelly Ford?"

"Bold as brass she was. She was shopping with him and she took him into that shop where my boyfriend had been attacked. They were all over each other. I couldn't believe it."

"You started to follow her?"

"At first it was just that I wanted to know where she lived. I intended to go and see her; have it out with her, tell her what I thought of her. I didn't quite have the courage though, so I'm ashamed to say that I ended up following her."

I raised my eyebrows. Moira was *ashamed* of following Kelly; how had she coped with the guilt of murder?

"And then one day I followed her to Huxley Point. She had a couple of bags with her and I guessed she had left home. I saw the young lad go in as well. I waited until the next time she went in and followed her on foot. She went to the top floor and when I got there there was no sign of her. I knew she must have gone into one of the flats."

"What about the first of May? What happened then?" I said, almost in a whisper.

"I decided to talk to her. See, when I'd been helped by Victim Support, one of the workers there suggested a kind of face-to-face reconciliation. I would meet the people who'd been responsible for Dan's death. We would talk. I should say what it had done to my life. They could say what it had done to theirs."

"I've heard of that," Joey said. "A couple of blokes that I knew in prison took part in it. They said it was a real shock to meet the people that they'd robbed."

"Right," Moira was nodding, "that's it. That's why I decided to go and see her."

She was speaking faster, hardly pausing for breath.

"I waited until the lad went out and I went up to the top floor. It didn't take me a minute to see which flat it was, there were marks in the dust, the padlock was different. I knocked on the door and I heard her call out, 'Coming!' She thought it was the boy-friend, coming back for something. When she opened the door and saw me her face dropped. She must have thought I was from the council because she started saying that she had rights to squat there and that I would have to go to court to get her out."

Moira wasn't looking at us any more. She was staring into the floorboards.

"I told her who I was and said I wanted to talk to her. She told me to clear off but she left the door open so I followed her in. She was jumpy, walking up and down. She asked me if I'd been following her. I tried to be honest with her and then she said that I'd been making phone calls. She said she'd go to the police and tell them that I was *stalking* her. You have to understand, I'd gone there to reconcile with her but she was talking non-stop, she was aggressive. At one point she accused me of wanting revenge; she said that I wanted to *kill* her."

Moira looked up at me and Joey.

"As if I could *kill* anyone."

I was puzzled. What was Moira telling us? I gave Joey a quizzical look but he was too busy concentrating on the story.

"She became hysterical. In the end I grabbed her by the shoulders and shook her hard. I was screaming, 'Shut up, you stupid girl! Shut up!' And then I slapped her across the face. It was a hard slap. I felt my hand stinging afterwards."

Moira started to cry. She crossed her legs and put her head in her hands. Then she carried on in a trembling voice.

"She was shocked. She stood still for a moment and then started to back away from me. I said, 'I'm sorry, I didn't mean to do that,' but she turned and ran out into the hall. I ran after her. I was afraid that she would tell someone that I had attacked her. When she pushed the front door open I went round her and stood in front of the lift and then the stairs, just to stop her running down. You see, it was all getting out of hand."

Moira's shoulders were shaking and she was rubbing her eyes with her fingers.

"She ran in the opposite direction. Up the stairs. At first I didn't know where she was going. I didn't know there was an entrance to the roof. I followed her and all of a sudden we were both out on top of the building. I stopped in my tracks. I shouted at her to calm down but I don't think she heard any of it. She kept backing away."

"She fell by accident?" I said, trying to imagine the scene.

"If I'd just left her there, if I'd just come back down the stairs and left her to calm down. But I was afraid that she was going to fall, so I walked towards her holding out my hand for her to come back to the stairs. It seemed such a tiny area. My head was going light; I'm not so good when it comes to heights, see? I was desperate to get off that roof and downstairs, but she just became more hysterical. She turned to get away from me and made a great lunge in the opposite direction. She had no idea how close to the edge she was."

"She ran off the roof herself," I said.

"One minute she was there in front of me. The next she was gone."

We all sat in silence. In my head there was a moving picture of Kelly Ford, hysterical, backing away from Moira, turning at the last minute to realize that she was too close to the edge, that it was too late to turn back. The momentum, like an invisible killer, pulling her off the roof and into the air.

"If it was an accident, why did you run away?" Joey said, bringing me back down to earth.

"I was in a state of shock. I knew it was an accident but somewhere deep down I'd always wanted to get revenge. For a long time after it happened I actually thought I had pushed her off."

"So you ran away?"

"I was calm. That was the amazing thing. I went back down to the flat and tidied up. I found the keys in the kitchen and locked up the padlock. I walked out of the building while they were still waiting for the ambulance. Nobody saw me. They were just looking at the body on the ground."

We sat there while Moira sobbed quietly.

"Why did you go to Mrs Ford? Why did you pretend to be from Victim Support?" I said.

"I didn't. I went to tell her what I'd done. When I turned up I said, 'I want to talk to you about how Kelly died,' and she said she'd been expecting me. After a few minutes I realized she'd thought that I was from the Victim Support agency. By then I couldn't tell her a thing. I kept putting it off, thinking I'll tell her next time. It just never happened and she came to rely on me."

Something was bothering me.

"If you didn't kill Kelly deliberately, for revenge I mean, why did you try to kill Carly Dickens?"

Moira looked at me, tearfully.

"I didn't try to kill Carly Dickens. I had nothing

to do with her accident. Don't you think one death was enough for me?"

Then she started to cry again.

After a while, Joey and I cleared up the tea cups and saucers and put the carrot cake back into its tin. All the time Moira sat holding her padded envelope close to her chest.

22
Confession

We took Moira Henderson to the police station. She sat in the front passenger seat and Joey sat in the back. We both felt sorry for her. Joey spent a lot of the journey giving her advice.

"It was an awful accident, you didn't intend to kill her, you were trying to stop her getting hurt. You must be careful not to incriminate yourself. I know the police. They can make you say things that you don't mean."

He gave the word *police* a heavy emphasis. Moira didn't answer. She just looked straight ahead. Joey continued anyway.

"You need a solicitor; you shouldn't give anyone that statement until you see a solicitor."

He was right. Moira needed to talk to someone

who knew the law. She *mmmed* at his words but her arms were tightly folded across the brown envelope and her legs were clamped together.

I wasn't sure that she would get much sympathy from the police. If only she had gone to them straight away! If only she hadn't pretended to be from Victim Support. That wouldn't go in her favour at all.

"I can understand how Mrs Ford mistook you for the woman from Victim Support. I can even understand why you went along with it that day. But why did you spend hours and hours with the woman? How do you think she'll feel when she finds out?"

Moira shook her head and spoke. Her voice sounded thick and croaky.

"I know it looks callous but it wasn't like that. Believe me, I didn't plan it, not at all. Mrs Ford was so wretched on that first meeting. That's why I couldn't tell her the truth. I stayed for hours and when I left she seemed a bit better. She made me promise to come back the next day. She even took my phone number and rang me the next morning. She needed me. Raymond was worse than useless. He just kept whining on and on about his loss. He didn't think about his mum."

"But didn't you think she would find out? Eventually?"

"Yes, but I thought she'd be stronger then. I just wanted to help her get through the first few days.

Then it became a week. Then it was just until the funeral was over. There never seemed to be a right time to tell her. In the end I decided to hang on until someone else found out the truth. I knew it was only a matter of time until someone discovered that I was Dan's partner."

I was quiet, letting it all sink in. There was some logic in her explanation. She'd been involved in death and deception and yet I found myself liking her. It was a strange feeling.

As we parked outside the station a police car pulled up alongside us, blocking the traffic. In the back of it was Des Murray. Sitting beside him looking disgruntled was Liam Casey. Des Murray wound his window down and leaned out.

"Have you done your statements?" he said, aggressively.

"Yes, and we've brought Moira Henderson in to speak to you!" I said, eyeing three cars that were queuing up behind the police car.

"I've got no time for that. I've got suspect number one here," he said sarcastically, pointing at Liam.

"Waste of time," I said. "I've got a woman here who says she was with Kelly when she fell off the roof."

Des Murray looked at Moira and then at me and Joey. He opened his mouth to speak but obviously thought better of it. There was the sound of a horn from some car driver down the street. He turned round and gave a look of fury at the driver behind who was holding his palms in mid-air, protesting his innocence.

"See me inside!" he commanded and tapped on the driver's shoulder to move off.

Des Murray led us into the main CID office. There were a lot of people milling about in there, some wearing badges and drinking from china cups and saucers. A notice on the wall said *Zero Tolerance – A Blueprint for the Future?*

"There's a conference based here," Des Murray said, looking pained. Moira Henderson and I found a couple of empty chairs and Joey perched uncomfortably on the edge of a desk, looking agitated. Around us were small groups of men in suits talking excitedly to each other.

"I'll be back in a minute. Then I want to know exactly what's going on here."

Des Murray said it suspiciously, looking directly at me, as though I had just committed a crime. Liam Casey gave me a look of consternation as he was led off by a WPC. It was becoming difficult to hold my composure.

From the far end of the room, beyond the groups of delegates, we could see a WPC edging through with Mrs Ford behind her. When she got closer I could see that Mrs Ford looked flustered, her jacket done up on the wrong buttons, her hair standing up as if she hadn't had time to comb it. Her face hardened when she saw me, but it softened again as soon as she saw Moira.

"Moira, I'm so glad you're here," she said, breathlessly. "You won't believe it but they've arrested my Raymond."

Moira didn't say a word. Neither did I. Mrs Ford would find out soon enough.

"Do you hear me?" she said, grabbing Moira's arm. "They're trying to put my Raymond in prison!"

I could see Des Murray coming back in. Liam Casey was no longer with him. He walked through the room stopping briefly to talk to one or two of the suited men. Then he came back to us, ignored Mrs Ford's presence and spoke to me.

"Now what's going on, Miss Kelly?"

"There has been a development," I said cagily, not wanting to go into details in front of Mrs Ford. "Can we talk in private?"

Des Murray sighed. He seemed on the brink of telling me off. Instead, he pulled me a little way away from everyone else and spoke to me in a weary voice.

"I am very busy," he said. "I've got Liam Casey in one interview room being questioned about Kelly Ford's death. I've got Raymond Ford in another for the hit-and-run. If you have something to tell me then I'd appreciate it if you'd do it quickly."

I gave him a look of extreme agitation and eyed

Mrs Ford. I could not bear for her to hear the truth about her daughter's death out here in front of everyone. It wasn't right. Des Murray finally realized and looked around at Mrs Ford. He spoke gently to the WPC beside her.

"Take Mrs Ford to the canteen for a cup of tea, dear, will you?"

Mrs Ford looked affronted. A couple of the conference delegates looked in our direction.

"No, you don't understand. I need to be here. It's important. You've arrested my son and he's innocent. You'll have to let him go now because Moira is his alibi. She was sitting with him that night. Isn't that right Moira?"

We all looked at Moira. She said nothing and was still clinging on to her envelope.

"Moira! Why won't you tell them? Don't let me lose my son as well as my daughter. Tell them he was with you!"

Those words seemed to wake Moira up and she pulled herself together.

"What is going on here, Patsy?" Des Murray said, a little tersely. "Have you brought this woman in as an alibi? I thought you said something about her being on the roof?"

But Moira had started talking quickly and Mrs Ford didn't seem to have heard what Des Murray had said.

"It's true, Raymond Ford spent that evening with

me. I'd gone to see Maureen but she'd been drinking heavily. Raymond said she was asleep in the back room. I ended up spending a couple of hours with him. He liked to talk about Kelly, you see, and I felt I owed him that much."

"Are you telling me that Raymond Ford didn't drive that car?" Des Murray said, perplexed. He looked like a man who'd just found a fifty-pound note only to lose it again.

And then it all made sense. Raymond hadn't driven the car that knocked Carly over. He had no need to kill Carly. Someone else did though. Someone who had found out about the anonymous phone calls; someone who had good reason to think that Carly Dickens might have killed her daughter. Someone who wanted revenge, pure and simple.

I turned and looked at the older woman. She was standing as close to Moira as she could.

"Mrs Ford, you drove the car that knocked Carly over," I said. "You thought that Carly had killed Kelly. You sat and waited for her to come home from work and when you saw her get out of my car you pulled out and deliberately ran her over."

"What?" she said.

Everyone turned to look at her. A dozen or so of the men in suits were looking as well.

"That's ridiculous!" she said, but her voice lacked conviction.

"Mrs Ford?" Des Murray looked at her.

Maureen Ford slumped against a desk and let her handbag drop on to the floor. A WPC stepped towards her and held her by the arm. In a couple of seconds she was crying into her hands.

"She killed my Kelly. She was getting away with it. I had to do something."

"Oh Maureen. It wasn't like that," Moira said, standing up and walking over to the older woman. "It wasn't like that at all."

Des Murray looked at the two weeping women and then at me. He looked as though he might burst with frustration.

"I just wish I knew what's going on!"

Within the next hour Des Murray had rearranged the people in his interview rooms. In one he had Mrs Ford and in the other he had Moira Henderson. Both were waiting for their solicitors. He put me and Joey in his office and asked someone to get us some tea.

Liam Casey had been released and so had Raymond Ford. I saw Liam through the office window being led out of the station by a WPC. She had her hand on his shoulder and was smiling at him and saying things with an apologetic expression on her face.

Liam had been an innocent bystander. He had suffered a loss and had grieved quietly without letting anyone know. I wondered if Victim Support would send someone to see him.

Raymond Ford was in a different position. Although he was innocent of the hit-and-run he had lied about it and tried to dispose of the car. Des Murray led him into the office where we were sitting.

"Look after him for a few minutes, will you?" he said.

Raymond sat meekly on a chair, his shoulders hunched over. He refused the offer of a cup of tea and just sat banging his knuckles together.

"Are they going to charge you?" Joey said.

Raymond shrugged his shoulders.

"They may not," I said, trying to look on the bright side. "They may not even charge your mum. They may take the circumstances into account."

"You mean my sister's death? You mean those *circumstances*," he said, nastily.

His face was a waxy colour and his eyes looked bloodshot. He had lost everything; his sister whom he loved too much and his mother whom he had tried to protect. I should feel sorry for him, I knew. He of all people deserved some sympathy.

The trouble was I had none to give him.

23
Keeping in Touch

A few days later I finished my letter to Billy. I spent some time explaining about the case.

Kelly Ford was one of those people who thought that she was always being bullied or picked on. Her brother had looked out for her but when she no longer needed him he became fixated with her, following her, keeping her things. Truthfully, he is a very odd character.

When Vince Black made threats against Kelly, it confirmed everything she had ever feared; that someone was out to get her. Carly's phone calls and being followed by a red car meant that Kelly was completely paranoid. It all goes some way to explaining what happened on the roof that day. A normal person would have dealt with it differently. Kelly just went to pieces.

What will happen to Moira Henderson? I don't think she'll be charged. She's still in a state of shock about losing Dan Mackenzie. On top of that she feels responsible for the death of a sixteen-year-old girl.

Mrs Ford has been charged with attempted murder. No doubt her state of mind and grief will be a powerful argument against prison.

So, it's all over.

The letter stretched over five pages. I'd told Billy lots about what was happening in my life but I'd left one thing out. In the end I had to mention it. I tried to be as honest as I could.

A couple of weeks after you left I ran into Joey Hooper. You remember him? He's been a real friend and has helped me with the case. He's really nice and I'm probably going to spend some time with him. He's doing his A levels and I said I'd help him revise.

I'd not told any lies but I'd not told the complete truth either. What was the point? I didn't know whether me and Joey had any unfinished business. I decided to wait and see before confessing anything to Billy. I printed off the letter and then read it through. In my own handwriting I added the last line with several large kisses.

I miss you lots. Love, Patsy.

I went out immediately and posted it.

Later on I drove to Heather Warren's flat. She had returned home the previous day and I was keen to see her. When I knocked on the door it took several minutes for her to answer. I wondered what state of mind she would be in.

"Patsy," she said, giving me a big smile.

She was wearing a track suit and her hair had just been washed. She looked more like her old self.

"I've just got off the phone to Des Murray. He said some very nice things about you!" she said, taking an electric kettle and filling it with water.

"Did he tell you he tried to arrest me?" I said.

"He mentioned something about it," she laughed.

She was too cheerful. Was she covering up her feelings about the miscarriage? Or was she really over it? I wanted to ask her, but I didn't have the courage.

When I'd visited Heather in hospital I had seen a different side of her; a more human side. She'd spoken to me in an intimate way, told me about her deepest feelings. She'd needed me. Now it seemed different. It was as though the window that she'd opened between us had been closed again. I wanted to say, *Do you think about the baby you lost?* But I couldn't. We were back to the old topic of conversation. The case.

"What I don't understand is how Moira Henderson was able to pose as a member of Victim Support without anyone noticing," she said.

"Apparently Victim Support had told Mrs Ford that someone would be round on the same day that Moira turned up. Mrs Ford thought Moira Henderson was that person. When the real woman turned up Raymond Ford answered the door and said that someone had already come. The woman from Victim Support assumed there'd been a mix-up. She went off home. She didn't bother to tell anyone. It was just one of those things."

Heather was opening and closing cupboards looking for something and I started to think about what I'd just said. *It was just one of those things*. A statement that covered many of the inexplicable mysteries of life. Why did Vincent Black start a fight in a jeweller's shop? Why didn't Dan Mackenzie go straight to the hospital? Why did Kelly go up on to the roof of Huxley Point? Why didn't the Victim Support woman check up?

"I hear that your mum and Gerry are getting married!" Heather's voice interrupted my thoughts.

"Yes, in two weeks."

"I take it you're not too thrilled," she said, placing a mug of steaming tea in front of me.

I shrugged. We both looked at each other. Heather had been involved with Gerry once and she knew my feelings about him.

"Be grateful, at least you're not a bridesmaid."

I laughed and drank my tea. Heather went to her desk and pulled out a folder and handed it to me.

"What's this?" I said, opening it up.

"Don't say no before you've even looked at it."

It was a bunch of leaflets about joining the police. I gave Heather a look of tolerance. We'd been here before. Heather was trying to talk me into giving up work in my uncle's agency and joining the police. It was something I'd always dismissed.

"Just think about it. You could be involved in investigations from the word go. You'd have all the resources of the police force at your fingertips. You could get things done instead of being on the outside all the time."

I held the leaflets loosely in my fingers, glancing at the WPC on the front. *Opportunities For Women in Today's Police Force!*

"I'll think about it," I said and shoved them all into my rucksack.

"You promise?" she said.

"I promise."

Later on that evening I sat in the kitchen while Gerry walked up and down modelling the suit he was going to wear on the day he married my mum. I was tidying out my rucksack in preparation for taking some books over to Joey Hooper.

"What do you think, Pats?" he said, holding the lapels in his hands.

It was an improvement. The dark colour and formal style made him look like a bank manager or a deputy head teacher. My mum was looking proudly at him, her hands clasped in appreciation.

"Do you think he'll make a good husband, love?"

"He'll do," I said. And I suppose I meant it.

They both giggled like teenagers and I sat watching them sternly like someone's disapproving mum.

At least I didn't have to be a bridesmaid. I had to be thankful for that.